LIVING PROOF
A Novel of Key West

KEVIN MAY

SUBTROPIC PRESS
KEY WEST
CONCH REPUBLIC

SUBTROPIC PRESS
P.O. Box 94
Key West, FL 33041

Cover: Todd Santoro

ISBN-13: 978-0615615905
ISBN-10: 0615615902

TRUTH CANNOT BE ACQUIRED IF NOT SOUGHT

LOVE CANNOT BE ATTAINED IF NOT SURRENDERED

PEACE CANNOT BE ACHIEVED IF NOT FREE

.prologue

I'm a dead man.

.01

"So what are you running from, stranger?"

The unanticipated interrogation of the barkeep made me recoil with an abruptness that nearly rocked me from the stool where I'd perched the past six afternoons. That, and being equilibrium challenged. A result of the five or so Captain & Cokes I'd already consumed on this, my sworn day of sobriety. In response to her inquiry, I merely offered a smirk.

"See, that's what you do. I've been watching you romance the tourists and locals alike and I have got to say, you are good. I've never seen anyone work an audience with such finesse. You pilfer through the intimate details of the lives of the unsuspecting while not giving up too much information about yourself."

"Just the way I like it," I freely confessed, admiring her style.

"And to think, at first I figured you were just another hustler we'd soon be running off the island. That's not you, is it? I can tell you one thing for sure—you are that guy. The one who's got something to hide."

I knew she knew she was right about me, on all counts. And from my experience, that's the last person one should ever choose to challenge. Having been scrutinized by the best, the insightfulness of this unassuming dealer of our social disease caught me completely off guard.

She likely overheard pieces of my tale while I was chatting it up with a variety of travelers, both foreign and domestic. I can engage them all. That's an advantage of being well traveled. I typically offer a local connection for most anyone who crosses my path. And by their very nature, people seek the security of familiarity wherever they go. Well, most people. Not necessarily those of us who've found ourselves at the end of the road.

What I'd gathered while observing her from across the altar on my daily pilgrimage to the Schooner Wharf Bar, this little cutie was likely your typical rebellious rich kid who had enthusiastically advanced into adulthood to eventually achieve the status of social outcast. Quite fitting for Key West, the island of misfit toys.

Her intellect was impressive, while her ability to charm rivaled my own. Yet she was encompassed by an aura of independence that appeared impenetrable. An alluring quality for an adventurer such as myself. However, it was her crystal-green eyes, that puffy little grin and the adorable sprinkling of freckles that dusted her sun-kissed cheeks that lured me to settle on this particular barstool at this peculiar bar to set up camp.

I had discovered this establishment on a journey to the Florida Keys some two-plus decades earlier and thankfully, nothing much had changed. The entire place, partially enclosed by an improvised tarp and tin roof, was little more than a compound of outbuildings linked by a scattering of worn wooden tables that surrounded a tired mess of a service area, constructed from salvaged materials given up by the sea. Festive mementos, yellowing photographs and an odd array of seemingly insignificant artifacts adorn her dingy interior. Stating a curious nautical quaintness, the Schooner Wharf's rough and rugged décor was ideally befitting the eccentric mix of local legends that daily lined her rails.

"It's Blake, right?"

I nodded while studying her eyes in an attempt to gauge her genuine level of interest.

"I'm Lacey, in case you didn't catch it."

"I caught it," I said, reaching across the bar to shake her hand. "It's a true pleasure to make your acquaintance, Ms. McKenna."

"Ms. McKenna? Now, how'd you know my last name?"

"Simply by paying attention," I said. "It's important I get to know the folks in my new hometown."

"I heard you were planning on sticking around."

"You heard?" I lifted my glass to indicate I needed one more.

"Didn't you know? There's plenty of speculation being tossed around, but you've got to take into account that Key West is a small town. Real small."

"Juicy stuff, I hope."

"Perhaps," she said, blessing me with an extra long pour of spirits. "So tell me, new guy, what's your story? On this island, if you don't get the truth out there first, the rumors are sure to fill the void."

News travels fast in a small town. Faster still when confined to a two by four mile island, a place of one degree of separation, two at the very most. Here, with Cuba closer than the nearest Walmart, gossip reigns supreme as the locals' favorite pastime.

Life's lessons had persuaded me to be tolerant of the rumor and innuendo that continually surrounded me. Mainly due to the fact I was deserving of such. Nonetheless, Lacey's words were a poignant reminder of what compelled me to this passage in the first place. I was faced with finally getting what I had always wanted out of life: truth. The angst that drove me to escape.

Spilling into the bar with a boisterous arrival were a crew of middle-aged men, adorned with a colorful array of silly, tropical-themed hats, crunching across the gravel floor in unison. That group of well-oiled rednecks poured up to the bar just as I was expected to come clean. I wanted to come clean. That had long been my intention. However, as duly warned, this island is too damn small for anyone to get away with anything. Being honest here would mean giving up my privacy, something I have always cherished. Far worse, there was a very real possibility that my candor could end up costing me my life.

Albeit one hell of a fun ride, from the day I signed on, my professional tenure had been draped in secrets and lies. A life of deception that perpetually cultivated more new enemies than friends. Yet starting over in this tropical paradise, I vowed to strip away the years of denial to face another painful truth: My entire adult life had been one big, strategic fabrication.

"Save me from the insanity, Blake." Lacey spoke with a sweetness that gently drew me back to the present. "All I needed to end my shift was one more bunch of sloppy drunks. I really can't wait for this day to be over. Mind if I close you out?"

Without waiting for a response, she turned to tally my tab. While she faced the register, I felt compelled to try a little simple magic on my new best girl friend. Some women find it captivating when I read them. Others find it a reason to run.

"So tell me, Lacey, which parent is the psychologist?"

"A shrink? Whatever gave you that idea, crazy man?" she asked, tossing the check my way with exaggerated force, and a wink.

I watched as she made her final rounds, saying good-bye and collecting her take. From where I sat, it was becoming quite clear Lacey had three things going for her: she was way too cute, way too smart, and appeared to have an interest in me. All qualities that demanded my undivided attention. Although I've long considered intelligence to be the sexiest of traits in the female persuasion, a capacity Lacey had sufficiently demonstrated, it was her playfulness that captured my intrigue. Pulling cash from the side pocket of my cargo shorts, I reviewed the bill—a thoughtful total of five dollars. I tossed down a fifty.

"That's sweet of you," I said.

"I gave you the locals' discount and my new friend special. Welcome to Key West. I think you're gonna fit in just fine around here."

"Thanks for the vote of confidence. Meeting you, I feel like I've made a friend today."

"I believe you have, too," she said, grabbing my cash off the bar. "Say, what are you doing later? I'm going out on a friend's sailboat. You should come along. Have you ever been sailing?"

I thought of giving a brief travelogue of the summer I was stationed in Oslo, Norway, where I had the privilege of learning the art of the wind and sails from one of the best. After further consideration, I decided to err on the side of caution. At times, my real life adventures tended to be taken as arrogant lies. "I can hold my own," I said. "Are you sure your friend won't mind?"

"It'll be just you and me. He has to work tonight and, as usual, everyone else petered out."

"I'd love to, if you're sure you want to trust a mysterious stranger like me all alone at sea."

Flashing a devilish grin, she jotted down her number on a Schooner Wharf Rolodex, the cardboard coaster intended to soak up the sweat of the drinking class. "Just don't you worry. I can take care of myself. You'll find that most of us down here have experienced life on the edge a time or two."

"Perhaps another reason this island feels so much like home."

"So Doc, I need to finish up so I can get out of here. Hmm, Doc. I like that. It fits. You're a smart guy. I believe I've just landed on the perfect island persona for you," she said, organizing her tips.

"Where should I meet you?"

"We'll be launching from behind the Half Shell Raw Bar. That's up the waterfront a hundred yards or so. Give me a call in an hour for my ETA. I gotta run home first to shower and stuff."

"That's a deal," I said, gulping the last of my cocktail.

"One more thing. Your question—it's was."

Anticipating my look of bewilderment she delivered her closing line.

"You asked which parent was a psychologist. It was my dad, but he passed several years back."

"I'm sorry." A true sense of empathy surfaced on my face. "There is something else that I should tell you."

"What is it, Doc?"

"I'm not running from," I grabbed her Rolodex card from the bar, "I'm running to."

.02

SUNDAY | 19 OCTOBER | 15:07 CST
Latitude = 44.4511, Longitude = -88.0611
Apartment of Jake Lander
De Pere, Wisconsin

Jake's darkened loft, dampened by the autumn chill and stale from days of vacancy, greeted Kendra with an overwhelming emptiness. That haunting feeling of abandon had consumed her long before arriving for this, their scheduled reunion. Standing at the entryway, his key in one hand and a celebratory bottle of champagne in the other, her prepared plea for forgiveness found no jury waiting. The dead silence of his space entombed her, making way for the first real tear she had shed in years.

It had been ten days since she last saw him. Ten days of no contact and no calls. That was the deal. His deal. For her, it was ten days of emotional hell. And anger, at him for not sending even one text, but mostly at herself for pushing him away.

Jake had insisted they take a break, *"Ten days, Kendra. You know as well as I do, both of us could use a little time apart."* Their situation had become complicated, as office romances tend to do. *"After that, hopefully we can get things back to normal around here. And this time, no sex!"*

Kendra could have justified checking in on him the day after their falling out. It was her duty. Yet her devotion to Jake, and her guilt over how things ended, required she respect his wishes and give him the time he demanded.

Love was a foreign emotion for Kendra, particularly when it involved true intimacy. Not that she lacked the physical attributes or charisma necessary to attract a lover. With fluid mocha hair that brushed her shoulders, a petite, fit build, soft and expressive facial features, all packaged in a rough and tumble country girl's exuberance, Kendra had captured the eye of many a man, and woman.

Her career took priority in life. At least that's what she had convinced herself of since graduating from Kansas State University eight years earlier. Insightful enough to know her mistrust only served to sabotage her relationships, she had yet to gain the wisdom to stop. The separation from Jake was all the proof she needed. This time she was prepared to fight for love.

Nine months earlier, Kendra had been assigned the case of Jake Lander upon his relocation from a Boulder, Colorado safe house to his new identity in the Midwest. An assignment she now realized could ultimately cost her the career she was willing to die for.

Their romance had played out much like their professions, full of intrigue, speculation and a fair share of maneuvering, each strategically guarding their personal territory. Although based on mutual respect and aroused by genuine chemistry, their love affair was regularly sabotaged by timing and mistrust. When one had mustered the courage to seal an emotional bond, the other was busy building walls. Their final showdown came on the heels of Kendra's careless declaration, *"Get over yourself, Lander. Seducing you was part of my assignment."*

Needing answers, she scanned Jake's surroundings for clues. His loft, a one-room apartment in a renovated circa 1890 tool foundry offered the idyllic old-world backdrop of rugged simplicity and exposed red brick walls to properly present his collection of contemporary artwork, a tangible expression of Jake's paradoxical nature.

Twisting open the blinds, the waning sunlight exposed the physical evidence of what she most feared: Jake was gone for good. The proof, tastefully presented on his black-marble dining table, was the relics of a twenty-five year career: his identification cards, laptop, credit cards, passports, firearms, and Blackberry.

"You son of a bitch! I'm not the one to blame. You used me!"

Standing alone in his space, Kendra realized, given Jake's disappearance, this was no longer a private matter. Their personal crisis had escalated into a critical professional threat. At this point, her only option was to make the phone call that would force her to reveal their affair and admit her failure.

.03

Arriving home, worn from her seventh consecutive day of work, Lacey dropped to her futon for a smoke and to steal some love from Sinatra, her aristocratic, tuxedo-wearing kitty. It was 4:45 and time for Roger's regularly scheduled call. Her cell phone buzzed on the coffee table. "Right on time. You ready for work?"

Detective Morales had chased after Lacey for the better part of a year. Their first encounter occurred while Roger was working a crime scene at Jimmy Buffett's recording studio on the waterfront next to the Schooner Wharf Bar. That nondescript white box of a building had been the scene of a burglary before day's first light. For Roger, it was love at first sight.

"Yeah, and if all goes as planned it's going to be a long night. How was your day?"

"Good. The crowd seemed to be in a tipping mood."

"Then you can pay for dinner tomorrow night," he said. "That is if nobody ends up murdered or missing between now and then."

"Real nice. Let's hope no one's personal tragedy disrupts your day off."

"So, what's the word on the street? Any rumors I should be aware of?"

"Nothing to report, sir."

"I didn't mean it that way, Lacey.

"You most certainly did."

"You're right. I guess I did," he said.

"I finally got a chance to talk with the new guy I told you about. He seems like a decent fellow, after all. Not some lowlife con artist or drug dealer like you suspected."

"Really. What's his story?"

"His name's Blake. I believe he's a retired businessman of some sort. Pretty young to be retired, so I figure he must have done well for himself. Interesting guy. He's sure kept the customers entertained all week with his stories. From the sound of it, he's lived one hell of an adventurous life. You'll have to stop in to meet him."

"You say it's Blake? What's his last name? Did you catch where he came from?"

"Leave it alone, copper. I don't need a background check on every new person I meet, thank you very much."

"Sorry if my job gets in the way of your good times."

"It's not your job to assume the worst of my friends."

"Now he's your friend? Lacey, you just don't get it. You don't see what I see on a daily basis. This island attracts the best of the worst."

"Can we drop it?"

After an uncomfortable silence, Roger said, "Are you still planning to take the boat out?"

"If that's still alright with you." Lacey knew where this was leading, but she had no choice. "Just so you know, I asked Doc, I mean Blake, the new guy, if he wanted to come along."

"Lacey, this new boyfriend of yours is beginning to piss me off."

"And you disguising your jealousy with concern for my well-being is beginning to piss me off. Tell you what, you're right. I'm asking too much. Why should you trust my judgment, let alone trust me?"

"He's a guy, Lacey! You know exactly what he has on his mind."

"You think I'm some little tramp, now?"

"Well, Lacey, I—"

"Really, Roger?"

"What do you want me to say?"

"Apparently I was wrong to think you'd rather I be honest with you. Tell you what, I'll just rent a damn boat from the docks."

Roger wasn't prepared for a showdown. Stubbornly digging in had cost him dearly in the past. "Lacey, take my boat and have a good time. I'm not worried about you. It's that guy. I have a bad feeling about him."

Sensing victory, Lacey didn't hesitate. "Thank you for trusting me, Roger."

"Still, you've got to respect where I'm coming from. Odds are your friend is a good person, but just to play it safe, take the pistol I left at your place."

"Are you serious?"

"I gave it to you for your protection, because I care. What in God's name is wrong with that?"

Choosing to avoid any more drama, and not wanting to risk losing access to his boat for the night, she conceded. "I respect that your paranoia is well earned, and you're right, we all get fooled now and again. I'll take your gun. Promise. Now I've gotta go get ready."

"Alright, but just one more thing. I've programmed my number into your phone. All you have to do is press and hold '1' for two-seconds."

"I remember, Roger. Will you please stop freaking out?"

"Okay. But Doc, is he a Doctor?

"Drop it, will you?" She walked over to the cabinet where he had put a .45 caliber Ruger. "I'm getting your gun right now." After using her index finger to briefly imitate a pistol to the forehead in a mock suicide, she grabbed his gun from the cabinet and tossed it on the futon next to her backpack.

"Be careful, it's loaded," Roger said, leaving her with an uneasy feeling that he was out there, somewhere, watching her every move.

"Listen, Rog, I'm going to run."

"I hope you guys have a nice time out on my boat. I wish I didn't have to work. I'd really like the chance to meet your new friend," he said, not able to leave well enough alone.

"Have a good night, Roger. Please don't spend your whole shift worrying about me. Everything will be fine."

.04

Oswald Reinbold, sitting in the study of his North Shore residence, had just finished the broadcast of a blowout of exasperating proportion: Chicago 3, Minnesota 38. Sundays were the only day of the week he took for himself. His sacred day of hibernation. This Sunday, given the performance of his Bears, little in the way of relaxation had been gained.

Serving as CIA Domestic Operations Officer and the Chicago Station Chief for over two decades, he was a well respected, stone-faced, naturalized citizen born in Germany to a World War II era barmaid, fathered by an unknown U.S. soldier.

Despite his foreign birth and slight holdover accent, Oswald had made his way up the ranks of the Agency rather aggressively while burning very few bridges in his ascension. Rotund, round-faced and balding, a solitary man in his sixties who wore a Buddha's demeanor, Oswald's sensitivity and awareness were the forces behind his success. Known for his calm nature and solid reasoning abilities, he had earned the respect of subordinates and superiors alike. Often assigned the challenging cases, he rarely let the stress of the job get to him. The Bears, on the other hand, were a different story.

While pouring yet another Maker's Mark to wash away the memory of the slaughter he had just witnessed, his business line began to ring. Oswald knew it would be sobering news. No one with that number would dare call on a Sunday if it were not. A glance at the Caller ID exposed the guilty party.

"Reinbold here. What is it Agent Carlin?"

"Sorry to disturb you. I wouldn't have bothered you if this wasn't urgent." Getting to the point, she presented him with the reprehensible bottom-line. "Jake has disappeared and I believe he's gone for good."

Oswald recruited Agent Kendra Carlin straight out of college and had been her boss, mentor and trusted confidant ever since. She was what he referred to as the ideal field agent for Midwest Operations when lobbying to bring her on board. A political science major with a minor in women's studies, Kendra's charming farm girl exterior conveniently concealed her impressive analytic abilities. Her brazen and, on occasion, lewd approach with men played exceedingly well in the middle states. She simply and quite successfully used her sexuality to accomplish the objectives of her assignments, an ability that seemed to give her a sadistically satisfying sense of power over the men she was assigned to manage or manipulate.

"What do you mean he's disappeared? Read me in, Agent!" Uncharacteristically red-faced, Oswald paused and sipped his Maker's Mark in an effort to calm his nerves. Reclaiming his composure, he focused on the facts. "When did he go missing?"

"That's the worst part, sir. I don't know. At the max, I would estimate no more than nine, maybe ten days."

"Ten days! You estimate?"

"For this to make sense, you need to know that I've fallen in love with Jake."

"Love? I thought you hated men."

"Of all people, I assumed you'd get it, Ozzy. You've sure as hell taken a great deal of personal interest in Jake. I've seen how you look at him."

Her insinuation regarding Oswald's sexuality was a cheap shot, his accusation regarding hers, a slap in the face. Both had gone too far.

Kendra tried to explain. "I didn't see it coming, it just happened."

"In all honesty, Kendra, I can empathize. Given the opportunity, I could have easily fallen into Jake's trap."

Stunned by Oswald's admission, Kendra scrambled to fill the void created by the candor of his words. "Getting back to the facts, sir, on the evening of Thursday, October 9, Jake, for reasons best left undocumented, requested an unofficial sabbatical from Agency supervision. As in, we split up and he needed time away from me. I knew what I was doing was wrong. I just thought—"

"Kendra, I get it, but what makes you believe he's left for good?"

Pacing the floor, Kendra observed Jake's monument to his desertion—the display of his tools of the trade, neatly organized on his dining room table. "Jake left literally everything. Even his Blackberry."

The smartphone Jake left behind was the only piece of evidence needed to draw such a conclusion. He lived with that phone attached to his person, night and day. As he often said when telling the tales of his international exploits, *"Two things I always keep the closest—a passport and my phone. You've got to have the means to get out and always, always gotta stay connected."*

"Damn him!" Oswald said. "He's finally done it. He's gone off the deep end. I knew I was giving him too much freedom."

"Oswald, you couldn't have known."

"I take responsibility for this debacle. I should have stayed dialed in," Oswald said before finishing off the remaining sip from his glass. "You realize it's imperative we locate him first."

"First, sir?"

"I haven't been completely forthright with you, Kendra. There's more to our problem than you know. Besides that, there's more to Jake Lander than you're aware."

"Why wouldn't you have provided me with his complete case history?"

"Simply an issue of need to know. Now you do. The protocol for Jake's case requires extreme measures should he do anything so ludicrous as go AWOL."

"How extreme?

"Under these circumstances, I'm required to impose a CoK on Jake Lander."

"Capture or Kill? Jake? Don't you think that would've been useful for me to know before now?"

"I couldn't risk telling you. The details of Jake's past are classified—closely held for his own safety. Well, and for that matter, the security of us all. I'll hold off informing Langley for as long as possible. Do you have any idea where he may have fled?"

"Who knows? Most likely where it's warm. Once the temperature started dropping up here, all Jake talked about was how much he hated the winter weather," she said. "I haven't finished my search of his apartment. Hopefully I'll turn-up something of a lead here."

"After you document his place, meet me at the office." Oswald peered at the clock on his desk. "No later than 2200 hours. Given the way you drive, that should be plenty of time." Rubbing the back of his neck in an attempt to relieve the mounting tension, Oswald considered their next move. "Kendra, you'll want to pack for extended travel. We'll be in the field until he's located."

"Will do. But tell me, sir. Why the CoK? What's Jake know that's such a threat?"

"I'll fill you in on what little information I have when we meet tonight. For now, all I can say is Jake's disappearance is not simply an internal matter. Once it becomes known that he's on the run, the Agency will undoubtedly classify him a national security risk."

.05

F inding a payphone that actually works these days is more of a challenge than one might think. A seemingly simple task, yet it offered a stark reminder that my life had become far different from what it was so very few days ago. Albeit liberating, exchanging your life for the real thing comes with its share of challenges.

By escaping to the Florida Keys, I had become what they feared most. Free. Free from the existence they had provided me in their finely tuned world of deception. Although that old life yielded all imaginable conveniences and unimaginable excitement, living a lie had grown tiresome. Deep within, I had come to conclude that no other choice remained. I imagined they were well aware of that sentiment, given my casual attitude toward our most recent arrangement.

They would have you believe me to be far from liberated. In all probability, they'd refer to my escape as something more along the lines of a self-imposed death sentence. They'd surely say I'd gone completely mad and this, my most recent rebel's stand, only served to substantiate their diagnosis.

From an insider's perspective, I believed my actions only served to prove one thing: I have always been a rogue participant in their plan to save me from myself. Regardless, I was over it, finished playing the game and adhering to the protocol. I was tired of living under their security, and worst of all, their surveillance.

Let me assure you, their concern for me was far from nobel. Given their assumptions were accurate, I'm a walking, talking threat to our nation's security. A fact that continued to amuse the hell out of me. Sure, I knew what they wanted. Something I could not offer. Never would I divulge that lie.

Considering, they deserved credit. They worked with me. They had plenty of reason to be frustrated with my rebellious actions while under their watch. But they hung in there. Not to mention, they did save my ass on more than one occasion. For that, I am eternally grateful. And to be quite honest, a couple of them were true friends, even though they could never know where I hung my bandana at night.

Moving about the harbor walk, overlooking a flotilla of ego and excess, I stopped to take in the natural beauty swirling around me. The week-long smile that ached across my face exposed my joy. Within my grasp was the life I had long dreamed existed.

I cherished the simple contentment I had discovered here. Key West was somehow magical in that way. The island didn't only encourage a come as you are attitude, from what I'd observed, it was required. As a newcomer, I was amazed at how easily the smile of a stranger could be turned into a friend. Emotionally honest and refreshingly open, locals took time to see the beauty in others. Should they not find any, however, you'd be sure to hear about it. As one well worn drunken sailor warned: *This town can chew you up and spit you out faster than any other port known to man.*

Locating another wretched contender for placing my call, I inserted my coins to thankfully receive a dial tone in return. Before dialing, the realization hit me: Tonight, while sailing the Florida Straits, Lacey would likely pursue the particulars of my past. An unwelcome confrontation that could expose my deepest desire—to risk everything for freedom. Thus my dilemma. At what price truth?

SUNDAY | 19 OCTOBER | 17:23 EST
Latitude: 24.5583, Longitude: -81.7874
KWPD Headquarters, North Roosevelt Boulevard
Key West, Florida

Detective Morales, obsessed with the thought of his girl out sailing with some other guy, unlocked the door to his unmarked Crown Victoria. Lacey's independence and her inner-strength were the core qualities that initially attracted him, and now frustrated him. Yet he knew, should he push, she would scramble away faster than a cornered iguana.

Roger had long proven himself to be a first-rate police officer. Regardless of the unyielding respect he had earned during his tenure on the force, a badge of dishonor, his family name, relentlessly tormented him.

Key West has seen more than its share of scandals over the decades, but the 1984 case involving Roger's Uncle Nestor undoubtedly holds the distinction as the most infamous. Referred to as the *Bubba Bust* by locals, then-police detective Nestor Morales, along with a cast of other Key West cops and characters, was investigated and eventually arrested by the FBI on federal racketeering and cocaine trafficking charges. The extent of the drug ring's illegal activities were so pervasive that the Miami Bureau of the FBI declared the entire island of Key West a criminal enterprise under RICO, the Racketeer Influenced and Corrupt Organizations Act. Roger, driven to cleanse the transgressions of the past from his family name, found it inconceivable to ever forgive his once-favorite uncle.

Waiting in the cruiser while his partner made her way through the palm tree lined parking lot to join him, he placed the key in the ignition and repeated his daily prayer.

Lord, allow me the courage to serve and protect with the wisdom of your ways. As I watch over others, watch over my loved ones, my partner and me. In your Holy Name, amen.

His partner and longtime best friend, Rosalyn Chapman, was, like himself, a Conch, born and raised in the Florida Keys. A woman of color, Rosalyn's roots dated further back, to the first Bahamian settlers on the island. She garnered a true sense of pride from that fact, which translated into a tremendous sense of duty as a Key West police officer. Together they were arguably the most respected team in the department.

"You know, Roz, dating the girl of your dreams can be a real nightmare."

"See Roger, it is true. Be careful what you wish for, you might get it." Rosalyn maneuvered the safety belt around her waist. "What'd Miss Lacey do this time?"

"Nothing really."

"That might be the problem."

"Maybe it's that I feel like she calls all the shots."

"You're the one in hot pursuit. That definitely puts you at a disadvantage."

"I guess your right."

"Besides that, you're the man. New love or old, the woman always calls the shots."

"I know, Roz."

"What'd you tell me last time? *No more insecure chicks!* Now you've got that pretty and smart and *not too girly-girl* you've been waiting for. The one who's got it all. Isn't that what you've been sayin'?"

Pulling from headquarters to begin their shift, Roger considered his partner's words. Lacey was just what he'd always pictured as the perfect second-in-command. "Maybe she doesn't need me."

"Really, Roger? Is that it?"

"It could be I'm not cut out for the independent type?"

"I don't know, but like I've been telling you, you need to lighten-up or you'll lose that girl."

"I need to lighten-up? Do you really think I'm that controlling?"

"Those weren't my words, but since you brought it up, give me an example where you believe you may have been controlling," she said, allowing Roger the rope needed to hang himself.

"Okay, like today," he blindly began tying his noose, "on my way into work, Lacey informs me she's taking that new guy along with her gang sailing tonight. On my boat!"

Roger was unable to see the red flag Rosalyn was frantically waiving in her head. Two weeks time had not passed since Roger spoke of Lacey's skillfulness at sea. *So capable, I told her she was awarded the privilege to sail the Lucky Dog anytime she likes,* Rosalyn thought, in a deep, authoritative voice. Now, with the new details of her partner's plight, coupled with her innate curiosity, Rosalyn redirected her line of questioning. "Who's the guy?"

"I told you about him. The new guy in town that's been hanging around the Schooner Wharf during Lacey's shift."

Rosalyn knew Roger could be a jealous guy. Trust issues had followed him since he was a child. His father left the island when he was young, leaving his Uncle Nestor to serve as the male role model in his life. Given the events of which Roger rarely spoke, Rosalyn had long been compelled to serve as counsel to her dear friend.

"You know, Rog, some couples, no matter how enamored or in love, just aren't good for one another. Now I'm not sayin' Lacey isn't the one for you. That's something you two need to figure out together. Still, you're responsible for taking care of your own shit first."

Rosalyn's words struck a tender cord. To alleviate the pressure Roger felt mounting, he went on the offensive. "So this guy, Lacey tells me he's a retired businessman who looks too young to be retired. That has potential drug dealer written all over it."

"Every new person that moves to town is a potential drug dealer to you, Detective."

"Think about it, Roz—"

Interrupting Roger's therapy session, their anticipated alert blared over the patrol car's radio.

Attention ops team. Operation Night Dive is a go. I repeat, Night Dive is a go. Immediately proceed to your designated positions. And hang tough guys; it's going to be a long, wet night.

.07

"Come aboard, mate."

There she stood at the helm of the Lucky Dog wearing sopping-wet braids of ginger and the face of an angel. With the blazing sun's reflection waltzing off the water to shimmer all around her in droplets of effervescent light, I knew I had just laid eyes on the next seraph to rock my world and ultimately break my heart.

Don't get me wrong. It's not that I assume seeking true love is a futile endeavor. I'm anything but a pessimist. However, I have passionately pursued true love my entire life. Damn good at it, too. So given my level of expertise on this matter, I'm well aware of the odds of ever finding the real thing. With that said, I'd never allow that sad fact to stop me from trying.

"Let's unleash this puppy." Lacey said, pointing toward the taut line linking the bow of the Dog to the dock. "You know the routine." Not wasting a second, she orchestrated the launch of Roger's well maintained 30' Catalina Tall Rig while orienting me on the vessel's safety features, emphasizing the location of fire extinguishers and life preservers.

"Nice breeze tonight. We couldn't have asked for better," Lacey said, combating the sputtering motor. "Once we're through the harbor traffic, it'll be sails up for the rest of the night."

Each evening on the island, a slight westward tilt could be felt as hoards of sunset worshippers congregated by the harbor's edge in anticipation of the legendary *green flash*. They would arrive to take watch by land, sea and air until the excitement would build to a crescendo of wake, song and revelry.

Key West's Sunset Celebration corrals the visiting masses at Mallory Square. There, rows of original art and wares, created by the local artisans that stood behind their transportable displays, likely peddled to the ritual by bicycle, surrounded rope-outlined stages that featured some of the foremost street performers in the industry. Watching those exceedingly talented few born of a special breed helped me to realize that life really isn't much more than a circus, not much more of one than of our own choosing.

About the green flash, it really does occur. Not that I could personally attest to its existence. That's an enchanting instant I had yet to experience. Without getting into the scientific jargon, the green flash is produced by a unique set of atmospheric conditions, which emits a brief but brilliant flash of emerald light at the precise moment the sun dips below the horizon. However, old seafarers have long claimed the green flash offers a slight breach in the heavens above, signifying God's hand of approval on those who share in its beauty. A divine blessing of sorts.

Cruising through the harbor, with Christmas Tree Island and Sunset Key just off the starboard and the City of Key West quickly passing off the port, Lacey skillfully navigated us through the busy channel southward toward open waters. The incessant tropical breeze blowing across my face expelled the sweat from my brow. Any remnants of the stress and worry I hoarded back on land was banished by the rhythmic sway of the vessel and the salty spray of the ocean. Escaping from the sights, sounds and stimulation of Key West to join the sweet solitude of a timeless freedom, drifting quietly at sea, Lacey cut the engine.

"From a distance, our island seems so insignificant," I said as we wafted beyond the tropically picturesque beach at Fort Zachary Taylor, nestled along the southwestern edge of the island.

"Like I told you, it's small, but it's far from insignificant. Now give me a hand with the mainsail, will you?"

As we tugged in unison, hoisting the sail, the Lucky Dog lunged toward the horizon.

"And getting smaller," I said, noting our now rapid retreat from land.

Next, I dutifully proceeded to the jib, jockeying the sheet until fully capturing the eye of the wind in a successful attempt of showing my worthiness as a first mate.

"These days it couldn't get any smaller," Lacey said. "But spending time at sea is the best way I know to wash away all of life's little demons."

"I know what you mean," I said, while in my mind visualizing thousands of tiny drowning devils between us and the shoreline. "Still, the open seas present its own throng of angry spirits to contend with."

"Not to mention those pesky pirates ready to jump aboard and steal your dreams."

I am undeniably seduced by the sea, particularly when tempted by the mysteries hidden in her depths. As a Scorpio, a

Water Sign, I possess a predestined appreciation for her ways, while still maintaining a wary respect for her. What lives lurking deep within her currents has eternally frightened the hell out of me. Regardless, I'm compulsively drawn to that which I most fear. Rare and beautiful, like water's appeal, Lacey radiated a captivating, yet puzzling allure.

"Water is where I've always found my salvation," I said.

"Is that what you're running to? Salvation. Salvation from what?"

"I guess to or from is simply a matter of perspective."

"Come on. Eventually you gotta tell me about your past."

"I've got nothing to hide."

"Then fill me in."

"The quick and dirty of it is pretty mundane. I moved here from the Green Bay, Wisconsin area, a small town not much bigger than Key West called De Pere. Wonderful people, but nowhere near enough stimulation for my liking. Not to mention, winter up there is Siberia-cold. Before that, home was just outside Boulder, Colorado. However, for the majority of my career I was based out of Virginia, in the D.C. area."

"You don't seem like the D.C. type."

"I wasn't, really. I wasn't stateside all that much. My professional life was spent bouncing between nameless locations in random regions of the world, some civilized and others, not so much. I would go wherever my talents were needed, stayed until they were no longer required, then gone. In and out like I'd never even been there. Which, come to think of it, sounds frighteningly similar to my love life."

"It's good to know you'll move along quietly when I'm through with you," she said. "Now I want the good stuff. Tell me, were you a hired assassin for the underworld or maybe a government spy?"

"You got me. As a matter of fact, I was a spy *and* a hired assassin."

"I knew it the moment I met you," she said.

"No, nothing nearly that exciting."

"The international lifestyle sounds pretty exotic to me, especially since I haven't been off this rock in so long," she said setting the ship's GPS to pilot the way, offering me her undivided attention. "What did you do?"

"I had an ongoing contract with a U.S.-based international consulting group. I worked as a profiler and negotiator, assigned to global projects with a wide array of business and governmental entities."

"That sounds exciting."

"Believe me, it was. I loved the jet-setters' lifestyle, staying at the finest hotels, dining at the trendiest restaurants, while sipping the rarest of wines at exclusive nightspots, and of course, sharing the company of the most fascinating people," I said. "That is, when I was assigned to projects in the more civilized parts of the world."

"What a life. Why'd you ever give it up?"

"I awoke one day feeling suffocated and unbearably tired of chasing the dollar and getting my highs from the next novel conquest, allowing wealth and power to be the shallow gods I strived to serve each day. So poof, here I am, running to, not from, a life simply lived."

Lacey's peaceful smile and eyes of empathy seemed to express her respect for my convictions. Perhaps, she too shared a fool's spirit, possessing the ability to believe in hope.

"Blake, what can I say? That was beautiful. No, touching. No, more like beautifully touching. I don't know what to say. You," she gazed deeply into my eyes, "you are so," again hesitating while taking my hand, "you are so incredibly full of shit! What do you take me for, sailor?" she said, breaking from her straight face.

"What? I share my innermost feelings and you responded by being a smart ass. Great way to build trust with a new friend."

"I'm just having fun with you, Doc. It's hard to tell when you're being serious and when—"

"And when I'm being deceptive? That's what you were thinking, wasn't it?"

"In a sense, yes. Not to be judgmental, but there's an unusual quality about you. I'm just trying to get a grasp on who you really are."

"Get in line. I'm the man people either absolutely adore or incredibly loathe from the moment we meet. I'm used to the accusations and assumptions that come with being that guy. Guess you could say I'm like seasoning on a fresh salad or salt in a fresh wound."

"I didn't mean it in a bad way. I'm on the side of those who find you adorable."

"You're not so bad yourself," I said. "That is, except for when you've got your guard up."

"You noticed."

"You seem happy with where you are in life. So why the defensiveness?"

"My life is not so neat and tidy as it once was. But when your whole world comes crashing down right before it drops out from under you, neat and tidy doesn't much matter anymore."

I hadn't expected that level of honesty. From the look on her face, neither had she.

"What rocked your world?"

"The year I moved here I faced the deaths of the two most important people in my life, my daddy and my husband. The details no longer matter, but the fallout lives on. One thing's for sure, it certainly changed the direction of my life. Coming down here, I've found something that I thought I'd lost forever. Me."

"I'm glad I found you here, too," I said as I wrapped my arm around her, pulling her close in an effort to comfort.

"That's enough of the serious shit. We're out here to have fun. The sun's just about to set," she said, breaking free from me to reach for her backpack. "Do you partake?" Lacey offered, pulling out a smoke. "Oh, you've got to answer me one thing. How in the hell did you know my dad was a psychologist?"

"That was my job. I'd assess an individual's verbal and nonverbal cues, combined with my rather keen sense of intuition, to determine their overall personality profile."

"Impressive, Professor. Do you profile everyone?"

"Only the ones who offer a particular incentive for gaining their trust," I said, eyebrows mysteriously raised.

"Blake, now you're creeping me out. What reason do you have to profile me?"

I sensed her terror as fear welled up in her eyes. An indication that my initial suppositions were accurate. This girl definitely carries some kind of secret. At the moment that was the least of my worries. Putting her back at ease with me was my prime concern. "I didn't mean to scare you. I'm really not some stalker-type, if that's what you're thinking. From the moment I saw you behind the bar, I knew I wanted to get to know you. Not just for what I saw on the outside, but the beauty I found on the inside."

"That's sweet, Blake," she said. "Sorry I freaked."

We sat quietly as the settling sun dipped deep into the western sky. As day turned to night, the only sounds were the winds rustling against the sails and the sea repeatedly slapping the ship's hull. Breathing in the salty air, I found myself worlds away from my old life.

"We have a full moon rising," Lacey said. "You cool with staying out a little longer?"

"Perfect. There's no place I'd rather be than right here, right now, with you."

.08

SUNDAY | 19 OCTOBER | 19:58 EST
Latitude = 24.5584, Longitude = -81.8770
Aboard Unit A-03 of the KWPD Marine Fleet
The Gulf of Mexico, 4.7 Miles West of Key West

"Detective Morales, are you still with us?"

Dropping the binoculars from his eyes, Roger exposed the guilty-glance of a jealous voyeur. "Lacey has me a little distracted tonight. But over there, see? I'm positive that's the Lucky Dog."

A modest flotilla of Key West police boats, the city's contribution to an armada of local and federal law enforcement sea presence, had settled into their positions. As confirmed by Justice Department intelligence, a substantial shipment of cocaine was expected to arrive from Mexico by submersible in the early morning hours. The joint operation team members of the Department of Homeland Security's U.S. Immigration and Customs Enforcement, agents from the Department of Justice's Drug Enforcement Agency, and the U.S. Coast Guard were prepared for an anticipated bust that would score their team the trophies of the smugglers' submarine, as well as their stash.

"You sound surprised. You knew she was sailing tonight."

"I know, but she should be heading back in by now. It's not safe."

"Seriously, Roger? We're hours from seeing any action."

"I just don't want her out here."

"You think she'll be any safer ashore with your suspect?"

"Real nice. Just what I needed to hear," Roger said, directing his binoculars back toward the Lucky Dog. "I only see two people. I thought she'd invited a whole group. Here, you look, Roz."

"No. Roger, you look. I've never seen you this bad before, and I am not approvin'. You need to get it together. We've got a job to do."

"That's it, I'm calling her. I need her off the water and out of my sight."

"Fine with me, Detective. Lord knows we wouldn't want the Lucky Dog getting caught in the crossfire."

Roger stepped aside to place his call. Rosalyn turned away, contemplating the spiraling meltdown she had observed in Roger since he began dating Lacey.

A repetitive ring continued in Roger's ear. "It went to voicemail! What in the hell is she doing over there?"

.09

Interrupting our solitude, Lacey's phone began to ring.

"I better see who it is. Pass me my backpack, would you?"

Grabbing her heavily loaded bag in the midst of an unexpected wake that tossed us starboard, I clumsily spilled its contents across her lap and on to the deck. With a pronounced thud, a pistol toppled across the topside. Instinctively, I scrambled to the deck, coming up with the object of immediate threat.

"Interesting. Do you always bring a gun along when you go sailing? Is it to fend off pirates, or for protection from me?"

"Please, let me explain. It's not how it looks. You've got to believe me. Because of you,"

Red flag!

"my boyfriend, see,"

Red flag!!

"he's a cop and this is his boat."

Red flag!!!

Fooled again in the game of love. I can read the intentions of international dignitaries, but not those of the cutie sitting right next to me. A boyfriend and he's a cop? That's all I need. Some jealous boyfriend with the reason and the resources to call me out.

"He wanted me to bring it, in case you turned out to be crazy or something."

"Well, if I go all psycho on you, your protection will be right here," I said, safely placing the pistol in a latched compartment at the helm. "Why would you ask me to come if you didn't trust me in the first place?"

"Doc, I'm sorry. I should've left it home. He pushes me to do things, things that just aren't me."

"Sounds like a real healthy relationship."

"I should have told you I'm dating someone. Not that I'd actually call him my boyfriend. It's only been a little over a month and believe me, it's going nowhere fast." She glanced at her phone to identify the caller. "It's him. I better check my voicemail to see what he wanted."

As she listened to the message, I considered my circumstances. I know the lengths some guys will go to maintain control in their world, and nothing could hit closer to home than a girlfriend. This cop could easily derail my plans for a future of anonymity on this island. Lacey was undoubtedly a rare find, yet possibly not worth the risk.

"We need to turn back," Lacey said upon pushing the end button.

"What's the deal?" I asked as she began grappling with the jib. "Here, let me help you with that."

"No, it's fine. I got it," she said angrily pulling at the sheet. "He saw us, the jerk. He's been using binoculars to spy on me."

"I'm the wrong person to give advice concerning another man, but given your reaction, this relationship certainly doesn't seem to be working for you."

Thankfully, I didn't take a cheap shot and refer to him as her jealous stalker, not really boyfriend. Besides, she appeared to be on the verge of mutiny without my assistance.

"You're right. It's not working for me. He's a great guy and all, but his control issues are making me crazy. I've been a free-spirit my entire life and no guy is going to take that away from me."

"I can see that."

"I'm not doing this anymore. He and I are going to dinner tomorrow. I'll deal with it then."

"Hopefully that means you won't be bringing a gun on any future dates."

.10

Running late as usual, Kendra called Oswald from the road.

"Where are you?" He answered, anticipating her excuses.

"I've only made it as far as Sheboygan. The weekend traffic leaving Door County heading back into Chicago is insane. I'm still a good three hours out." Chugging the last of her Double Shot espresso drink, she said, "You know the Milwaukee highway construction bottleneck has got to be a real nightmare tonight."

Oswald had spent the time since her last call contemplating the day's disastrous news while combatively chasing those thoughts with whiskey. He mumbled into the handset, "Second thought, I have a better idea. Why don't you come here to the house? I really don't bewieve it would be wise of me to dwive into the city tonight. Besides, we don't need to attract attention by swiping into the office on a Sunday."

Never had Kendra known him to be one to over indulge, particularly to the point of slurring his words. It was then she realized that Jake's disappearance had not only shattered her world, but also played havoc with Oswald's sense of calm and balance.

"Are you all right, sir?"

"Hell no! I'm not all right! Our jobs are on the line. Don't you get it?"

"I get it, but if you hadn't had your head so far up Jake's ass, maybe you'd been a better mentor for me—bitch!"

Oswald shivered at her use of the expletive. *What? Next she'll be calling me a queen?* Rational or not, he had long feared his fetish with the Queen Mother and her fashions would one day be found out.

"Listen, Kendra, we're both far too emotionally involved with this one. We've got to pull it together. Jake's life is on the line."

Since her last call, the possible scenarios presented by Jake's disappearance had haunted Oswald, as did his admission to Kendra. It wasn't that he distrusted her. It went much deeper than that. In light of the truth being spoken, the cloak he had donned his entire life had become increasingly suffocating.

Oswald had taken a personal interest in Jake once assigned his case years earlier. Their association began at an Agency safe house outside of Porto, Portugal when he was charged with the responsibility of relocating Jake back to the States. Typically such high-ranking personnel would not travel for the retrieval of a rogue agent, but Jake's circumstances were unique.

Jake's case file, now scattered across Oswald's imported black mahogany desk, hand-selected in the Orient, was a blotted mess of censored pages, documents and photos. Practically the only identity not concealed in his dossier was that of Jake Lander, himself.

Even at Oswald's rank, he was not given unfettered access to the details of Jake's previous assignment, specifically in regard to the threat Jake posed. He was, however, well aware of the protocol should Jake go missing. *Only under the most extreme circumstances does the Agency resort to killing one of its own,* he often obsessed.

Though Jake remained an invaluable asset to the Agency, Oswald was told his final assignment played out as an international fiasco, resulting in his classification as a significant security risk. No further particulars were gleaned from those documents, nor from Jake's mouth. The best intelligence he had obtained paired Jake with a secret society based in Lugano, Switzerland. One whose objectives were believed to pose a threat to the American way of life.

"I'm sorry for calling you a bitch, Ozzy. I didn't mean to lash out at you like that. Jake has me totally freaked out."

"I'm right there with you. I honestly believe he'd allow me to assassinate him before returning on his own free will."

"We're not going to let that happen," she said. "I documented every square inch of his place and sent you an email with the photos attached. Hopefully there's a lead in there somewhere."

"I'll go download them."

"Oh, and sir, I did note one thing that was glaringly out of place. The cover page of a document sticking out of a safe in his bedroom closet. What I could fish out before it ripped had an intriguing title." She flipped open the file folder laying on the passenger seat, briefly running off the road in the process. "Have you ever heard of a report entitled, *Correlates of the PAS and DNA: Implications in Bioengineering and Societal Management?*"

"You said the PAS?"

"Yes, P - A - S.

"Did you get a photo of the safe before pulling it free?"

"Of course I did, but what do you believe is its significance?"

"Knowing Jake, he left it there as a clue, or simply to toy with us."

"And the PAS?"

"The Personality Assessment System, a creation of the late CIA Chief Psychologist, John Gittinger. I'm sure you've heard of him. His theories are central to Agency profiling operations to this day."

"His name, yes, but not the PAS. Remember, my specialization is strategic analysis. Besides, psychology has always scared the piss out of me."

"You are familiar with Project MK-ULTRA, aren't you?"

"Sure. The mind control research the Agency conducted decades ago."

"The Agency prefers to call it behavior modification," Oswald said.

"Whatever they called it, when it became public it was a real mess for the Agency. Weren't there Congressional hearings on the matter."

"Yes, and if you recall, John Gittinger was one of the Company employees questioned before that commission. However, it was Agency Operative Dr. Sidney Gottlieb who headed-up the research using Gittinger's theories at the core of MK-ULTRA experiments. Of more interest to us, Gittinger was the individual responsible for recruiting Jake Lander into service with the Agency."

"What, Jake's involved with mind control? No way he'd go that far."

"Kendra, I don't know what to think."

"This is a little much for my head to take in while dealing with this traffic. Tell you what, drink some coffee. I'll get there as quickly as I can. And Oswald, no more Maker's Mark."

SUNDAY | 19 OCTOBER | 21:29 EST
Latitude = 24.5584, Longitude = -81.8770
Pepe's Café and Steakhouse, 806 Caroline Street
Key West, Florida

"Cool place," I said, working my way around the sprawling tree growing through the center of the restaurant, "but tell me something." I directed Lacey's attention to the television hanging behind the bar. "What is it with the Weather Channel around here? Seems there's more weather bars than sports bars in this town."

"We do love that we're living in paradise, besides it's a seafarer's town. The weather impacts how people make their living around here. That, and then there's the folks who live out on the hook. When you take a dinghy home each night, you need to know when to leave."

"Which I would imagine also applies to a sea dog's alcohol level before hitting the skiff."

"You got that right. More than one drunken sailor's body has washed ashore down here."

We took the last two open seats at the bar, canopied by a sprawling Bougainvillea and surrounded by locals and their dogs. Another oddity of this town. Companion animals are welcomed at most local hangouts and many workplaces.

"I've never settled anyplace long enough to get a dog," I said, "but maybe it's time I do."

"What's that? Get a dog or settle in?"

"They'd go hand-in-hand, now wouldn't they? But seriously, I feel like I've finally found a place I could call home."

"That feeling doesn't fade over time, either. It only grows stronger, like an addiction," she said.

Our conversation had remained light since Lacey retrieved the voicemail from her beau aboard the Lucky Dog. Now off his boat and in the comfort of neutral territory, the time had come to continue on our journey of mutual discovery. It was my turn to ask the questions. My curiosity had been most aroused by her defensiveness. With the banter of humor, Lacey consistently deflected nearly every personal topic I posed. I wanted to know why. Insight into the *whys* of a person's life can be most revealing, however, they also possess the power to unleash pervasive pain.

"Out on the water tonight, I noticed you get flippant whenever the conversation becomes a little too personal for your liking. Which appears to be almost every topic."

"Humor has always been my defense mechanism. At least that's what my daddy always told me."

"So you've had a lifetime to perfect this talent."

"I wouldn't call it a talent, more like a bad habit. I'll try not to be so evasive, but be gentle with me."

Lacey reached over to grab a couple menus. I watched as she nervously wiped them down with a bar nap. Once they were apparently clean enough, she handed me one, opening it for my review. As if to hide, Lacey held the other menu close to her face.

"How about family? That's a relatively neutral subject for starters," I said.

Peering over the top of her emotional barricade, Lacey said, "I don't know about your family, but mine is far from neutral."

"Really? You speak fondly of your dad."

"He was the ideal father. He made me the person I am today. The good qualities, anyway."

"And mom?"

"My dad raised me," she said, the menu again blocking her eyes from my sight.

"Did I hit on another subject we need to avoid?"

"No, I can talk about it. Mother split the scene before I was three years old. Haven't heard a word from her since. I figured that meant she didn't want to be found, so I never looked."

"That had to be hard for a little girl to understand," I said, pulling the menu downward to look into her eyes.

"Dad tried to console me by telling me her problem wasn't us, but the demons inside her."

"As difficult as it may be to grow up without two parents in the home, there are times when it's actually a blessing."

"Believe me, I know. Kimberly should never have been a mother, or a wife for that matter. Dad said she was a master manipulator. Between her addictions and the lies they breed, she was incapable of maturing beyond the point of only thinking of herself. That's all I know. Can we move on?"

Having held out long enough, it was a good time to direct our conversation to the issue of the boyfriend, my *antagonist de jure*. "Sure. So why don't you tell me about this guy, what—"

"I was wondering how long it was going to take for you to ask. What's his name, right?"

"Well, actually yes."

"What is it with you guys? You always need to know the competition's name."

"Still, you'd better tell me his name so I don't have to refer to him as your *jealous stalker, not really boyfriend.*"

"It's Roger, or Detective Morales if you prefer. And he really isn't that bad a guy."

"That's exactly what I've always looked for in a soul mate: a not that bad a girl."

"You think you're cute?"

"I told you I'm the wrong guy to offer advice on this one."

"No advice needed. I'm sure Roger's also coming to the realization that this relationship isn't going to work. Of course, I'll give him the opportunity to admit it first. Otherwise, he'd end up blaming you for our breakup."

"I like the way you think."

"What about you? Who's the woman in your life, or is there one in every port?"

"There really haven't been that many ports over the past several years. Well, except for the one I just walked away from."

For the first time since skipping out on Kendra, I thought of how I ended it, and how it must have hurt her. Guilt management had always been one of my strong suits, a talent that was apparently slipping away. My heart ached for her. Those feelings unleashed a flurry of thoughts I found difficult to decipher. She was just a fling. I knew that going in. Considering her past, not to mention her cunning ability to get exactly what she wants out of people, I could never trust her in a committed relationship.

"The one you just walked away from?"

"It was similar to the one you're dealing with right now. Only ours took months to finally be put to rest."

"What happened?"

"She was, well, simply not that bad a girl. And for me, only a soul mate would warrant giving up my freedom. Regardless, I keep the faith that there's someone absolutely perfect on that horizon of my life."

"I admire that, Doc. It's refreshing to be around a man who hasn't given up on hope. Tell me more about, what's her name?"

"Uh, uh," I said, glancing up from my menu.

"I liked you better as the suave spy guy."

"Sorry. It's Kendra. But that's in the past where I want to keep it. My only concern is that she'll come looking for me."

"You owe her money or something?"

"No, I'm not a thief, either. Nor do I bring a gun along on my dates,"

"A date? Is that what this is?"

"No. But should that Roger-guy ever break your heart, I'll be here to offer a shoulder for you to cry on."

Providing us with a moment of levity, a small faction of French tourists politely pushed and shoved their way up to the bar, likely to soon be disenchanted by Pepe's wine selection.

"There it is," Lacey said. "Number Ninety-Nine of the reasons I love this town. Who'd have thought Key West would be such an international destination?"

"Of all the places in the world I've traveled Key West certainly has to be one of the friendliest places I've been."

"That's right, you're a traveling man. Just how many countries have you visited?"

"Not all of them, but pretty damn close."

"Travel is a love of mine, too," she said. "My favorite places were Amsterdam, Barcelona and, of course, Paris. That's where my daddy took me for my Sweet Sixteen."

50

"Those are some of my favorites, too."

"That life must have been incredible, always on the go, experiencing different cultures, and the food."

"It was amazing, but it came with its own brand of drawbacks," I said.

"Like what?"

"Like, that world never allowed for a dog, or for that matter, any other companion."

.12

"I absolutely hate that boring-ass drive," Kendra said as she burst in the side door of Oswald's 1970s contemporary lakefront home. Laden with a black canvas bag overstuffed with evidence hanging off one shoulder and her knapsack of personal effects slung from the other, she released her load in one simultaneous drop. Next, she struggled to peel off the pea coat from her sweaty body. "I don't know why I wear this thing. It's so itchy. Phew, I can tell you've got the fireplace stoked tonight. Smells great, but can we crack open a window? It's hot in here."

"Excuse me for saying so, but you look a wired mess," Oswald said.

"I believe I might've overdone it with the caffeine. When I get stressed, I gotta have my fix."

"Just how much synthetic speed did we shoot-up on the drive down?" Oswald chuckled to cover his sincere interest in Kendra's level of Java-induced insanity.

"I only had a couple cans of Double Shot Espresso. Well, I also backed it up with a super-sized Mello Yello I grabbed at Mickey-

D's; it washes away that stale coffee taste. Probably a little too much, huh?"

"How can you be so good at your job, yet such a train wreck when it comes to your personal life? You defy all logic, girlfriend."

Kendra considered, in light of Oswald's recent confession, his life defied the identical principle. *Did he really just call me girlfriend? He better not think he can start that gay talk with me. But it is amusing to see this side of the old Ozball.* She giggled aloud, hoping Oswald wouldn't ask. *It's probably healthy for the old boy to finally release some of his—gayness!*

"What are you smirking at? Now, just don't you start, missy" Oswald said with hands on hips, which only served to further encourage Kendra's complete meltdown.

With tears of emotional relief streaming down her cheeks, Kendra broke out in irrepressible amusement. "You, Oz. Now everything you do or say seems gay! I think I'm going to pee my pants."

"It would serve you right."

"You know I'm the last person who would care where you poke your thing. In all honesty, I'm honored you trusted me enough to come," she said, hesitating in an attempt to contain herself, "out of the closet!" She failed. "I'm going to the potty."

Joining Oswald among the organized clutter of his dimly lit, oak accented study, having finally gathered her wits, Kendra was prepared to get down to business.

"Okay, MK-ULTRA. Given Jake's age, the timeline doesn't fit. That project was dropped in the Sixties or Seventies, wasn't it?"

She said settling into Oswald's comfortably worn, brown leather sofa. "Jake would have still been a kid."

"You've always been gifted at spotting the discrepancies in a story."

"To be perfectly honest, what I shared with you from the road is the extent of my knowledge of that operation. I don't get how the details of a project that ended decades ago would have any relevance to Jake's current situation. But the mention of that report sure seemed to spark your interest."

"It did, and the photos of his safe. It appeared staged to me. Jake would never be so disorderly."

"Anal as hell, if you ask me," Kendra said.

"He left it there for a reason. You know there's an element of Jake Lander that wants to be found out. He leaves clues, his calling card. Frighteningly similar to a characteristic commonly found in the profile of a serial killer."

"He does the same thing in his personal life. I figured it was his way of maintaining some sense of independence."

"That safe was Jake's way of leaving us a message," Oswald said. "I'm sure of it."

"Maybe the clue was intended for me, communicating that he took off for a reason other than me."

"Kendra, you know he's a lone wolf."

"I know. I knew it from the start and still let down my guard."

"Well, I don't envy you. I'm beginning to think life is simply sport to Jake. Another game to win regardless of the odds." Oswald pointed toward a large stack of file folders on the corner of his desk. "Since being assigned Jake's case, I've spent literally hundreds of hours researching his past assignments, as well as his associations within the Agency."

54

"Examining the volumes of Oswald's compulsive labor, she said, "You're obsessed with Jake."

"Tell me the mysterious Agent Jake Lander doesn't pique your passion for intrigue. Don't you want to know why he's so politically toxic? He's a national security risk, yet not considered expendable."

"That doesn't mean you're not obsessed with him."

"Regardless of what you think, I believe that safe may hold the answers we're looking for." Oswald turned to his computer to enlarge the photo's thumbnail to full-size. "It's a bottom of the line model, not too heavy to move and easy enough to cut open once we get it back here."

"Before you even suggest it, I'm not about to make that trip a second time tonight. I've got his laptop. Don't you think examining its content would be a logical first step? I've obtained most of his passwords."

"I give you credit, you didn't let your heart cause you to completely abandon your responsibilities. I do find it rather fascinating that you can carry on a love affair with the man you're charged to manage. How you must thrive on having the upper hand."

"Frankly, that's one of the reasons I'm so good at my job. Except, this time I got played at my own game. Who knows, maybe I was ready to get played."

"You chose the wrong man to fall for."

"As you were quick to remind me of earlier today, I have men issues. And while we're on the subject, is Jake aware of your feelings for him?"

Kendra busily logged on to the laptop in an effort to avoid eye contact, Oswald sat back in his chair to consider her question.

"I certainly hope he doesn't. He definitely reads people better than anyone I know. Surely I would have picked up on it."

"He'd never let on if he did."

"You do realize my personal life is classified."

"The last thing I'd do is out you in the Agency."

"I have to admit, I've felt like a new person since coming out to you."

"This is going to take a while," Kendra said, eyeing the computer screen. "Fill me in on MK-ULTRA and Gittinger."

"Given that Project MK-ULTRA officially ended in 1963, you were correct in your assessment that Jake's age does not coincide with the timeframe. However, from my findings, the Agency's efforts were simply restructured and moved forward under a different code name."

"And the association between Jake and Gittinger?"

"Gittinger, who by the early Eighties shared a frightening likeness to that of Colonel Sanders, had long since retired from his post as CIA Chief Psychologist. Although, as it is with the Agency, the minds of Company employees are forever the property of the federal government."

"You said Gittinger was the operative who recruited Jake."

"Yes. How they became acquainted, I don't know. The earliest records I've located confirming their association date back to 1985. At the time, Jake was assigned to support one of the Agency's research installations at a small educational institution in rural Southeastern Ohio, called," Oswald rustled through the files on his desk, "here it is: Hocking College. That's where he received his field training in the PAS under the guidance of one of our best, Dr. Roxanne DuVivier. She was his first handler. He's always needed one."

"And this relates to Project MK-ULTRA how?"

Oswald leaned back in his chair as he began to brief her on one of the Agency's biggest, blackest eyes.

"As you know, the Agency was formed following World War II to coordinate espionage activities against the emerging threat of Communist Russia. With the fall of the Nazis, a wealth of German scientific knowledge came up for grabs, some of which was acquired through research methods not even the Agency would be willing to engage. I'm referring to the intellectual capital of the German scientists. This resulted in a race to recruit the best minds. Between us and the Soviets, literally thousands of German nationals were identified and relocated to either country."

"You're getting to MK-ULTRA, right?"

"Patience please, Kendra. As I was saying, following the war, armed with the scientific expertise of their acquisitions, the Agency was charged with Americanizing the German's research. This was conducted under a project code named ARTICHOKE. The intent of the Agency's original efforts under this initiative was to develop interrogation techniques to be applied to Russian spies."

"What kind of techniques?"

Pulling an interagency memo, dated January 25, 1952, from one of the files on his desk, Oswald read from the document. *"The objective of this initiative is for the evaluation and development of any method by which we can get information from a person against his will and without his knowledge. The methods employed in this research includes the use of drugs and chemicals, hypnosis and isolation."*

"That makes waterboarding sound like child's play. But you said that was carried out under Project ARTICHOKE. What about MK-ULTRA?"

"ARTICHOKE was the forerunner to the far more deviant MK-ULTRA." Flipping through the pages in a manila folder with the project's cryptonym handwritten across the tab, Oswald retrieved another Agency memo dated August 14, 1963. He adjusted the lamp to better see the blurred letters resulting from an overrun of copies made on a mimeograph machine. Reading aloud, he said, *"The mission of Project MK-ULTRA is to conduct research advancing avenues to the control of human behavior."* He scanned the page for other pertinent details. *"This will include the use of chemical and biological materials capable of producing human behavioral and physiological changes."* Continuing farther down the page, Oswald highlighted the fields of science that were exploited by this undertaking. *"Approaches will include the use of radiology, electro-shock, various fields of psychology, psychiatry, sociology and anthropology, graphology, harassment substances, and paramilitary devices and materials."*

"You can't be serious."

"Most certainly am."

"We're talking the torture and brainwashing of American citizens," she said.

"Here, get this. *Research in the manipulation of human behavior is considered by many authorities in medicine and related fields to be professionally unethical."* Oswald wiped the sweat from his forehead. "They knew what they were doing was wrong!"

"We usually do," Kendra said, walking to the window of Oswald's study that overlooked Lake Michigan. In an effort to temper the distasteful subject matter, she slid open the window for fresh air.

"Their research included the use of drugs, including LSD, covertly given to unwitting Americans. Agents would literally dope people in bars and drag them back to the safe house for study. That's one of the milder forms of atrocity that was performed by CIA personnel under the guise of MK-ULTRA. I'm not even going to get into the bizarre sex-based experiments they conducted."

"Sex experiments? Fun days to have been an agent," she said. "Now Gittinger, where does he fit into the picture?"

"Gittinger was a player, in that his theories of personality were central to the operation. A truly brilliant man, Gittinger single-handedly created a functional theory of human development and behavior predictability. His hypotheses on human intent and expected behavioral patterns continue to be the basis of Agency supposition to this day. Not only did he develop the theory, he masterfully supported his assumptions with an ingenious equation that draws from the subtest scores of the Wechsler Adult Intelligence Scale. Through his wisdom and wizardry, Gittinger established a formula that flawlessly pinpoints the psychological makeup of a given subject."

"From test scores?"

"Derived from what Gittinger termed the Personality Assessment System, or PAS, a comprehensive psychological grid of an individual's innermost motivators and their unique set of thought and behavior patterns could be acquired, thus determining a stimulus-response model of that subject."

"In English?" Kendra said.

"It means, armed with a subject's PAS profile, the trained individual can classify, with amazing accuracy, a person's *modus operandi*. In counterespionage, that translates into the use of an individual's PAS for the sole purpose of exposing and exploiting their weaknesses. In the interest of national security, of course."

"I recall being given the Wechsler when I entered the agency. Does that mean they did a PAS on me?"

"They do a PAS on every new agent."

"Are you privy to my results?"

"I am."

"Well, are you going to tell me?"

Oswald's mind raced, questioning if he should. He had it committed to memory. However, there are times when knowing too much about one's own psyche can have a debilitating impact. In Kendra's case, he assumed that would be the situation.

Kendra's childhood was marked by a rarely present, ever-drunken mom, accentuated by the lack of an earnest father figure. Often left to find her own way, Kendra sought refuge from life's hurt by busying her mind. She found intellectual pursuits kept her thoughts well organized and focused, as well as an effective way of preventing unwanted thoughts from re-emerging.

Sadly, Kendra was not always left alone. There were the other times when she was cursed to face what she now only relived in her nightmares. Apparently appearing more mature than her years to far too many of her passed-out mom's late night visitors, Kendra consequently encountered the deviant sexual maneuverings of the male species far too early in life.

Oswald was aware Kendra's environmental influences in childhood, coupled with her psychological predestation, indicated a high probability of promiscuity for pleasure, purpose or profit. That, along with a host of exceptional intellectual qualities held by only the best of agents, molded her into the idyllic government funded prostitute. *The most intimate secrets are always shared in bed*, he considered while glancing back toward Kendra.

"I don't know, Kendra. Not now, anyway. We have more important issues to deal with. Hand me the cover page of that report, will you? The title alone provides us with a definitive date stamp. DNA research was still in its infancy in the Eighties, which coincides with the timeframe I presume Jake's and Gittinger's association began. All this suggests that Gittinger's research has continued into more recent decades, and apparently, the Agency's interest in mind control."

Kendra located the torn cover page in her stack of evidence excavated from Jake's loft. "Here you go. The name of the author was lost in my attempt to fish it out."

Oswald reviewed the studied the cover page. Marked in bold print across the top, the words *Top Secret* verified the level of risk involved with looking too deeply into Jake's past.

"The top secret designation coupled with the subject matter of this report helps explain why Jake's Protocol calls for a Capture or Kill order."

"I don't get it."

"This would not be the first time the Company disposed of an agent associated with Gittinger's work. Does the name Frank Olson sound familiar?"

"Sure. Agent Frank Olson, the Agency researcher who flipped out on LSD and jumped to his death from a New York City hotel window."

"Only Olson didn't actually jump. He was silenced."

"Silenced?"

"What they said around Headquarters at the time was the guy woke up one day with morals and could no longer stomach the job."

"I can see why." she said.

"Many of the files related to the Olson case have since been declassified. They're freely available online—a real thorn for the Agency and the White House."

"For us, and the White House?"

"Two of the most powerful people from the George W. Bush administration are known to be directly linked to the cover-up of Olson's murder."

"President Bush? No way."

"No. Not W, but pretty damn close. Frank Olson's family was finally awarded a settlement of three-quarters of a million dollars directly from the Office of President Ford. That was no small bankroll back in 1976."

Kendra googled *Frank Olson + Ford White House.* Thousands of results were returned in a fraction of a second. "Where would we be without the Internet?"

"In some ways, far better off."

"You are so old-school." After landing on a couple useless results, her eyes zeroed in on an article entitled, *White House Cover-up Exposed by Ford Presidential Library Documents.* She quickly scanned the page for highlights. "Cheney, and Donald, too?"

"Both men were in the White House during President Ford's Administration. At the time of the Olson affair, Rumsfeld was White House Chief of Staff and Dick was an assistant to the President, and Donald's sidekick.

"Proof, leopards don't change their spots," she said.

"All things considered, I'm convinced Jake's involved with mind control research."

"And that means Jake's a dead man."

"Kendra, our only hope is to talk him back before this matter blows wide open. That would not bode well for any of us."

"Great, so he's going to take us down with him."

"We need that safe. Don't worry, not tonight. Both of us could use a little shut-eye."

"Thank God."

"I'll email the office to let them know we'll be conducting a weeklong working retreat at my home. By we, I mean you, me, and Jake."

"Everything we've talked about tonight only offers hints to why he left, not where he may have gone."

"You might want to take another look at the photos before you go to bed. As we've observed, Jake leaves clues. Perhaps the pointer will come in the form of what's not in the picture. Something meaningful or symbolic that he removed."

"Oswald, am I going to lose my job over this?"

"No, as long as we find him. Now get some rest. Your room is ready and the coffee pot is set to go for morning."

"One more question before you turn in," Kendra said. "Ozzy, are you in love with Jake?"

"Probably not. Perhaps more in love with what Jake embodies for me, and his zest for life. That, and, well, those who are unavailable are safer. Jake is simply an icon I've invoked to place my dreams upon. The imprisonment of impossible love is a comfort zone I have never mustered the courage to escape."

.13

Drunkenly tripping along the sidewalks of Old Town with Lacey nestled by my side, I blissfully whistled the theme song from *Popeye the Sailor Man* while reflecting on the marvelous evening we'd shared.

"So, sailor, I take it that means you had a good time on the water. I'm so glad you decided to come."

Following our dinner at Pepe's, a stroll along Duval Street for some late night people watching and window shopping led us to Lacey's favorite nightcap venue, Virgilio's. Located a few steps off the main drag, concealed behind an unassuming alley entrance, this secluded tropical garden bar is known for its eclectic mix of live music offered nightly. For romance and dance, there was no better hideaway on the island. Tonight's gig, a hot Latin band out of Miami, had us on our feet all night.

My dance moves had been perfected with the aid of a petite Portuguese princess I'd met years earlier while living on the other side of the Atlantic. Salsa, much like the Latin lovelies who intuitively know how to play their way into a man's heart, is a frantic dance of seduction. Although Lacey's knowledge of the precise steps was limited, she successfully faked her way deeper into my desires with each twirl and caress.

"Didn't you promise me just a nightcap? Yes, I definitely recall you saying thirty minutes tops. One of us has to get up for work in a few hours."

"Who was the one that didn't want the night to end?"

"It's been years since I've had that much fun. This is the best first date I've ever had."

"I'll toast to that. Then again, I really don't think I could handle another martini. Good thing Virgilio's closes early on Sunday nights."

"You call two o'clock on a Monday morning early? I see island life has already diluted your ability to reason. That's the first symptom of Keys' Disease. Between the sun and the suds, you've got to be careful. Combined, they'll fry your brain."

"Thanks for the warning, but I came prepared to face my demons."

"Well, you'll find them all right here waiting for you. Key West is the Garden of Good and Evil."

"More good than evil, I hope," I said. "Mind you, I've been to Eden. It's one of the most awesome manifestations of beauty one could behold, only to be hideously stained by her depravity."

"What in the hell are you talking about, Doc?"

"I'm talking about Eden. That was the code name for my last overseas assignment, and the reason I landed here."

"Now you've got me even more confused."

"I was stationed in Lugano, Switzerland, a place often referred to as Paradiso."

"Let me get this straight. You were stationed in Paradise, assigned to a project code named Eden. Who in the hell were you working for anyway? Good or evil?"

"If only our world were so black and white," I said.

"It all sounds a little too mysterious. You being straight with me?"

"I haven't lied to you, yet."

"No lies, simply avoiding the truth?"

"Like you're doing?" I asked.

"Fair is fair, Doc. That is, as long as you're not a wanted man. I'm not into playing cops then robbers."

"I'm no criminal. Are you?"

Offering comic relief at just the right moment, the sound of screeching wheels preceded a lavishly dressed gent pushing his upright piano down the center of Simonton Street, singing of a piano man's woes at the top of his lungs.

"Don't you just love it? Reason Number Twenty-Three: Our Eccentric Characters," she said. "The quirkiness of this town never grows old."

"And?"

"And, you're not going to let me off without answering, are you?"

"Nope."

"I'm not a mass murderer, if that's what you're getting at."

"Interesting. And?"

"And, that's all you're going to get tonight."

"Then let me ask you this. Would I be correct to assume that neither of us would want to be found?"

"I'd say that's a fair assumption," she said.

With arms linked and hands tightly grasped, we continued our seemingly endless trek northward on Southard Street. I pondered her evasiveness. Was she merely being playfully mysterious, or covering for a dark past?

"Where are you taking me, girl?"

"Love Lane. Don't worry, we're almost there."

"Seriously? You live on Love Lane?"

"At least it's not Poorhouse Lane. We've got one of those on the island, too."

We journeyed down the dimly lit alleyway to reach Lacey's place, a narrow wood-framed structure of Conch-style architecture, where Love Lane dead ends. Locating her keys, Lacey struggled with the lock. With a solid thump of the deadbolt, the door swung open to expose our welcoming committee, Lacey's cat, speaking with a voluminous purr.

"This is Sinatra." Lacey reached down to capture her elusive friend. "Right after I moved in here Sinatra started hanging around. We've been best buds ever since. Haven't we, old boy?" Lacey expressed her affection with a playful kiss on Sinatra's nose. "Do you like cats?"

"They're cool, the coy little fuzz balls."

"I'd ask you in, but my alarm clock will be going off way too soon. I'm filling in for Smythers at the bar over the next couple of days. Stop in to see me. I'll be there both days until four o'clock."

"You know I will."

"I had a wonderful time tonight, Doc. I hate to admit it, but you're making this break-up with Roger a lot easier. Hopefully we can end things without causing too much harm to one another's ego."

"I dread those talks, especially when I'm the one doing the leaving."

"Breaking hearts is nasty business," she said.

"Yes it is."

"Now I've got to get some sleep. Thanks for everything, baby. You sure know how to treat a girl."

We embraced farewell. Lacey momentarily nuzzled her head against my chest in a show of peaceful surrender.

"Okay, now go," she said.

.14

Flinging open the station door, Rosalyn called out to her partner. "Hey Roger, hold up a minute."

Roger had intentionally rushed to the parking lot without saying good-bye. After a grueling night on the water the only thing he wanted was his pillow.

"What's up, Roz?"

Catching up to him at the end of the walk, Rosalyn said, "I wanted to speak with you about last night."

"Can we just drop it? I know what you're going to say, so you can save your breath.," he said, yawning with guilt. "I'm painfully aware how inappropriate my behavior was and I'll deal with it on my own."

"Simmer down, white boy. I'm not here to jump your shit. It really wasn't that big a deal. I'm just worried. I've never seen you so," Rosalyn hesitated, "well, quite frankly, out of control."

"I know I've been off my game a little, lately."

"More than a little." Softening, Rosalyn said, "I'm just saying I'm here if you need to talk."

With Roger, Rosalyn demonstrated the shrewd astuteness afforded those women culturally scarred by a heritage of oppression. After successfully raising two fine young men, and happily running off one not so good one, she was well equipped to handle any emotional issue the male species could imaginably encounter.

Her boys barely knew their dad, which from Rosalyn's perspective was a blessing. More like an uncle than a father, Tyler's infrequent visits were disruptive at best. By the time her boys had reached puberty, she made the difficult decision to cut him completely out of their lives. She was not about to allow his despicable drunken, drugged and carousing lifestyle influence her little gentlemen.

Well respected throughout the community, Rosalyn exemplified the essence of the hardworking career woman and devoted single mother who successfully managed both sides of life with grace. She had created a secure and loving world for her boys, consistently filled with hugs, yet gilded in tough love. From an early age, she taught her sons the divinity of respect—*respect for God, respect for self and respect for others*. A lesson that had carried them through the many pitfalls faced while at war with maturation.

As for a special someone in her life, Rosalyn didn't have the space or the time that would dictate. Nor the patience. Working along side Roger served as a constant reminder.

Roger found solace in Rosalyn's practical words of wisdom whenever he reached wit's end. Now, with Lacey, he had undoubtedly arrived at that point.

"Roz, I've come to the conclusion that Lacey isn't the right girl for me, after all. She's everything I've ever dreamed of, except she brings out thoughts and feelings in me that are downright exhausting. At church yesterday morning, I actually asked God if Lacey had been sent into my life on a mission to totally muck everything up."

"You mean, preventing things from fitting nicely into those little boxes you've built your world on?"

"Is that what I do?"

"You're a wonderful man, but seriously, you can be so damn rigid and self-contained. Did you ever consider that maybe Lacey was sent into your life to offer you a chance to grow? The qualities that challenge us the most in others can also teach us the most about ourselves."

"She challenges me, that's for sure. As much as I'm drawn to her, I feel equally daunted by her. Then I get jealous and end up wanting to change her. Even I know that's not healthy, or even possible."

"Could the problem be you don't trust yourself?"

Roger stood perspiring under the heat of the raging morning sun, holding tightly to a *'Patrol Cars Only'* sign for stability. The awkwardness of the moment was amplified by the appearance of two fellow officers passing on their way from the parking lot. Roger would be devastated should others on the force catch wind of the difficulties in his personal life.

"I don't know. Lacey told me I keep my feelings so deep inside that I can't see the impact they have on my life. What do you think she means?"

"Didn't you ask her?"

"No, I was afraid to. Lacey's dad was a psychologist, so she thinks like a shrink. Hell, she usually knows how I'm going to react to a situation before I do."

Rosalyn saved his feelings by not pointing out how transparent he actually was. "That's something you need to discuss with her."

"Not only that, Lacey says I can be harsh when it comes to people's shortcomings. That I expect too much. I try to always be fair in upholding the law."

"You're the one who's always said, *I expect nothing more of others than I expect of myself*. And Roger, you hold yourself to a pretty high standard. You're one of the good guys, but like all of us, you've got room to grow."

"Plenty of room," he said.

"While we're on the subject, you are way too damn hard on yourself. Here, feel this." Rosalyn led Roger's index finger down the deepening crease centered between his eyebrows. "That forehead shouts tension. Something is eating at you and I'm starting to think it has very little to do with Miss Lacey."

"You're right. Something is eating me. Why can't I figure this out?" he said. "Am I losing it?"

"No, Roger. I believe this time you just might be on the verge of finding it."

"Finding what, Roz?"

"Yourself, Roger."

15

MONDAY | 20 OCTOBER | 09:42 CST
Latitude = 42.2096, Longitude = -87.8922
U.S. Interstate 94, Tri-State Tollway
Bannockburn, Illinois

On the road back to Jake's loft, Kendra had grown increasingly impatient with Oswald's questionable driving ability. The continual rhythmic lunge of his Mercedes Benz S-Class, marking Oswald's unsuccessful attempts at maintain a constant speed, was one of the numerous reasons she preferred to drive when they traveled together.

"That's a gas pedal, damn it. Not a drum pedal. Would you please use the cruise control already? I'm getting whiplash over here."

"Perhaps I should have let you drive."

"Maybe next time you'll listen."

"I wouldn't mind so much if you'd only spend some money and buy a dependable vehicle," he said, referring to Kendra's decrepit, yet dearly loved Ford F-150. "How old is that piece of junk you drive, anyway?"

"Critter will be fifteen next spring," she said, "and at least my piece of junk, as you call it, is American made. Not like this flashy foreign status symbol you choose to drive."

"Critter? You are such a little country girl."

"I'll take that as a compliment."

"It's not that I don't like Critter, I simply don't appreciate her interior's resemblance to that of a dumpster behind the local Starbucks. Do you ever throw any of those cups away?"

Kendra, having already sucked down an oversized tumbler of coffee and a couple Cherry Pop-Tarts, coaxing her to fully awaken, snapped, "I'm going to recycle those cups one of these days, if it's any of your damn business."

Minimal sleep had been acquired at Oswald's place. Tossing and turning, Kendra spent the hours scrutinizing the possible scenarios of Jake's desertion. With each new sequence of events diagramed on flowcharts in her mind, she repeatedly arrived at the same conclusion. The probability of a positive outcome was minimal, at best. She no longer perceived her personal loss of real consequence. With Jake's life hanging in the balance, she was faced with the most crucial, albeit unofficial, mission of her career: To save Jake Lander from himself.

"Ozzy, I've evaluated every imaginable outcome and even if we are the ones to locate Jake, I have to assume the worst. In the end, he's surely a dead man."

"What are you saying?"

"Think about it. There's no way he'll freely return to the Agency, nor does he have access to the resources necessary to successfully fall off the grid."

"We've got to do something," Oswald said. "Think. Who may have had contact with Jake over the past week?"

"Only one person fits that profile. Jeremy Brown."

"His friend who owns the wine bar. I remember him quite well. Is he—"

"No. I know what you're thinking and I assure you, Jeremy Brown is not gay. Sorry to disappoint, you old *hornball*. He can be a little over the top, but what do you expect? He's a musician," she said. "I know for a fact Jeremy loves his women."

Oswald fired back, "Sorry to disappoint you, but he's a little too hairy for my liking. Excuse me if that's too over the top for you. And just how, may I ask, do you know he prefers women, for a fact?"

"Don't be insinuating I slept with him. I'm in love with Jake, and I'm no slut, either."

Oswald's attack on her moral character drove Kendra to withdraw. Gazing out the car window, a growing sense of remorse encompassed her. Not just over the loss of Jake. Her jaded past was becoming ever more present, as well.

"Can we focus on the matter at hand?" Oswald said.

"Please."

"Two questions: Do you think Jake would have told Jeremy Brown where he was going and would Jeremy betray the confidence of his friend?"

"If Jake were to tell anyone, it'd be Jeremy. Those two hit it off like brothers from the moment they met. However, I honestly doubt Jake would share such delicate information with anyone. Also like brothers, if Jake did tell him, Jeremy would take it to the grave. That is, unless he thought Jake's life was in danger."

"I see where you're going with this," Oswald said. "You certainly are at your best when playing the heart strings."

"I'll need more coffee before planning my attack on Mr. Brown's sympathies. Will you hit the next exit? Besides, I really gotta pee."

"I'm a little hurt he didn't talk this over with me first. Jake should know he can trust me."

"And he likely also knew, if you couldn't talk him out of it, which is nearly impossible once he sets his mind to something, you would feel personally responsible should anything bad happen. Jake would never let you take on that liability."

16

MONDAY | 20 OCTOBER | 11:31 EST
Latitude = 42.1879, Longitude = -87.7874
La Casa Cayo, Whitehead Street, Unit A
Key West, Florida

"Good day, sir. Rise and shine. You're about to sleep away another gorgeous morning," my personal butler cheerfully announced, rousting me from the peacefulness of my dreams. "It's 11:30," he said with the enunciation of a proper Englishman, most befitting a gentleman's gentleman.

Kelley had been in my service for merely a week, yet proved to be a quick study. A master of subservient attentiveness, he was aware of my every move while anticipating any need that may warrant. Watchful for my return home at night, Kelley woke me each new day, only once I had acquired sufficient rest.

"Your coffee, sir," he said, placing a corrugated cup from Circle K, containing my precise blend of strong coffee, two percent milk and not too much sugar, on the nightstand. "And your morning paper, Blake." He gently rested a neatly-folded, pre-read copy of *The Key West Citizen* next to my head, which happened to be subconsciously hiding under the sheets.

"Thank you, Kelley."

"If I may say so, you were in a rather jolly mood upon arriving home this morning. Somewhat similar to a drooling dog in heat," he said. "May I ask, what is the name of our latest love of a lifetime? If it's none of my business, I'll just scurry along and leave you to awake in solitude."

Kelley was certainly justified in his evaluation of my nightly discoveries of passion. As it is with just about anyone who breaks free from the chains of bondage to seize newly acquired freedom, temporary anchors are commonly found to be of comfort.

"Lacey," I mumbled from under the sheets, looking up at the petite, white-haired gentleman boasting a matching beard. A proficient smart-ass, Kelley had already learned how defenseless I am in the morning hours. He seemed to delight in prodding the delirium I experience at that hour of each day. "Anything interesting in the paper this morning?" I asked while reaching for my morning buzz.

"The front page story did catch my eye. Anything with cheerleaders in the headlines assures a titillating story," he said, shaking imaginary pom-pons in the air as he wiggled his hips.

"Do tell." I said, burning my tongue on the steamy brew.

"The Key West High School cheerleading squad made it all the way to the state finals this year. Oh, those silly darlings. It seems some of our Key West cuties got caught smoking pot in their hotel room. The judges disqualified the poor little dears."

"Go Conchs!" I responded while still in a sleepy fog, frantically blowing across the top of my coffee cup in almost erotic anticipation. "Was there anything in the paper about a big coke bust in the Straits last night?"

"It wouldn't make it to press until tomorrow's paper. *The Citizen* is put to bed far too early to capture news from the previous evening. The *Coconut Telegraph* certainly seems to be working fine. Apparently you've heard the news before it hit the papers."

Sitting upright by this point, I stretched away the night, rubbing my eyes in an effort to focus. "Apparently," I said.

"I can see we still need a few minutes before joining the rest of the living. I'll leave you to your own devices."

"Good idea. Thanks for the coffee."

"Before I go, could a poor old soul bother you for twenty quid? It seems I've already spent this week's allowance. I needed to buy dog food for Scruffy. It's not her fault we're homeless, you understand. I'd feed her before eating myself," he awkwardly tugged at my heartstrings. "It's such a lovely day not to get out on the town. I'd so enjoy an afternoon treat over at the 801 Bar."

He helped himself to the cash strewn across my dresser. "I'm going to take a couple of these, too, if that's alright with you," he said, pilfering my pack of smokes.

Perhaps I should back up and start from the beginning. As is so often the case in life, things are not always as they appear.

Settling in a new location for an assignment that required I be on the sly, there are two factors I consider when making living arrangements. First and foremost, locate a place that does not do a background check. The second, a place that offers the lowest possible security deposit. In the low rent districts, I've found one rarely sees that money again. Either the super is a slime ball or there are times when circumstances dictate leaving on a moment's notice. Under either scenario those dollars are lost forever.

On the morning I hit town, a quick scan of Craigslist led me to La Casa Cayo, a locally infamous rooming house on Whitehead Street. The ideal place, offering a month-to-month rent option and a security deposit that was within reason. Ideally located in a hectic area, halfway between the Hemingway House and the Southernmost Point, I could easily be concealed in the company of the masses.

As it has been with almost everything in this town, my introduction to Kelley was a bit peculiar. Daryl, the building superintendent, introduced us after concluding the business of signing a rental agreement, handwritten on the back of a plumbing invoice that was likely not going to get paid any time soon. Daryl assumed, "You seem like a good guy. I'm sure you won't mind. Kelley and Scruffy stay over here."

He directed me but three steps from the front entrance of my new lair. Expecting to see a couple of pups chained up in the side yard, I stepped back in astonishment at the sight of Kelley and his beloved companion, Scruffy, atop a shabby, old army cot. Their home was the narrow margin of dirt and rubble that lay between my room and a dilapidated, six-foot tall cedar fence that protected us on the inside from outside's invaders.

No disrespect intended and none deserved, Kelley was a homeless man. Nor was I misleading in my assessment of his expertise as a steward. To hear Kelley tell it, after nearly three decades of employment as manservant for a family of Park Avenue aristocrats, one day, out of the blue, he was informed that his services were no longer required. Understandably devastated, he ended up without a job, direction, and ultimately, his self-dignity.

He now considers this island his last stop on the long and weary journey home. Like Kelley, due to circumstances beyond their control, or perhaps a few too many vodka tonics along the way, many a lost soul has found solace in this paradise, peacefully awaiting death's beckoning.

Kelley took obvious pride in that his services were once again required. Passing time in the confines of a boring life is much more bearable when one feels needed. I did need him. More than that, I trusted him. So, for around ten dollars a day, plus a few smokes and leftovers from the previous night's dinner, Kelley managed the more mundane aspects of my life.

His first assignment was to serve as my security advisor. Along with the bag of summer clothes I'd packed in preparation for this long awaited departure, I also brought along a rather large aluminum suitcase filled with a few significant remnants from my past. Also in that case was a sizable stash of cash that I had stockpiled over the years with this exact intention in mind. With the fervor of a miser, I had carefully concealed hundreds of one-hundred dollar bills under the pictures in volumes of photo albums memorializing what appeared to be family, old friends and past loves.

Spinning the case's duel combination locks to innocently offer proof that its contents were of little to no consequence, I explained to Kelley, "It's just a bunch of old memories and my research papers—family genealogy stuff. The case locks when shut. Being inaccessible, it would likely be too tempting for the super to pass up. Any idea where I might secure it?"

Affectively over dramatizing the fact that he was thinking, Kelley placed a finger to the side of his forehead. "I know the ideal place. When the torrent rains become unbearable, I crawl under the house for shelter. The opening is right next to my cot. I could easily keep close watch on it for you there."

"Perfect." I trusted Kelley and all, but I'm far from naive. The case alone would bring a hefty payoff at a pawnshop. "Is there anything substantial down there I could chain it to?"

"A cast iron sewage pipe is but a couple feet from the entrance. I could lock it up quite securely for you there. I'd be more than happy to visit the hardware store to pick up a lock and chain."

"Thanks, Kelley, but I came prepared," I proved by pulling a New York City-proof bicycle lock from my bag. "Show me where it is. The chain is so heavy, the lock is a real pain to get closed. Best if I do it."

With Kelley happily on his way to the bar with my money and smokes, and my cup of coffee a tolerable temperature for my lips, I was primed to take on a new day.

The morning light often brings clarity to my wandering soul. Today, particularly. My week of frolic and folly, a self-allotted holiday of debauchery, had officially come to a close. That salty dog's warning of this port's affinity for chewing up the best of men weighed heavy on my mind. As did what to do with my newfound freedom. A life of simple leisure was something I had long dreamed of conquering. Now that I had it, I needed to learn what to do with it.

Rationalizing, due to the fact I don't completely trust my own feelings, let alone anyone else's, I questioned the validity of Lacey's value as a potential partner. Of more consequence, did I even want one? A change of heart, or a fear of commitment? Either way, I'm notorious for over analyzing my feelings when it comes to romance. Lacey was delightful. But with her cop boyfriend, or even a soon to be ex-boyfriend who's a cop, the risks were too great. Then there's the issue of the Ruger. — *Be the snail*, I reminded myself.

Having completed my weeklong drunken orientation to paradise, I needed some alone time. Kayaking the mangroves promised such serenity. Not to mention, the best bet for keeping my butt out of the bars for the day.

17

MONDAY | 20 OCTOBER | 12:47 EST
Latitude = 24.5610, Longitude = -81.8019
Schooner Wharf Bar, The Historic Seaport
Key West, Florida

Awaiting the passage of hurricane season atop their preferred corner stools at the locals' end of the bar, Rita and Captain Gus leisurely consumed away yet another day. Like many a Key Wester, this couple personified a modern-day version of the pirates that once sailed these waters—living on the hook, anchored a good twenty-minute dinghy ride off shore. The Gypsy Rose, Captain Gus's beloved 41' Morgan schooner, was their home and Rita's safe haven.

"Only one more week until the Captain and I launch our annual winter voyage to points south and warmer climates," Rita said, just as she had counted down for the past several weeks. "Winter in the Keys is far too cold for my blood," she reminded all who cared to listen.

Rita was a tender and fragile flower, remarkably well disguised by her tough exterior and brusque demeanor. Years of tending to the tragedies of life as an ER nurse had contributed to her emotional abandon, but it was the self-imposed guilt over her personal failings that had trapped her inside a bottle of rum.

As she freely shared, *"I've survived the deaths of the three most important individuals in my life: my sons. One to a drug addiction, another to suicide, and the last, to our country fighting in Iraq. A mother should never have to experience the loss of a child, let alone all of them."*

The only place Rita felt sheltered from her demons was adrift at sea, under the watch of her Captain. It had been a decade since she first stepped aboard the Gypsy Rose for a drunken one-night stand. That indiscretion was the consummation of what developed into the longest relationship she had ever maintained. Gus, Rita's senior of fifteen years, was her one true love and solid rock.

Captain Gus Matheson, with sun-stained skin of leather, observant blue eyes, and a thick silvery mane perpetually drawn back in a ponytail, was a seasoned and fearless seafarer. Known to be a scrappy force to be reckoned with when cornered, he, like Rita, was better known for his compassion.

He knew Rita depended on him for her very survival, and at times her sanity. Yet, to hear Gus tell it, in his distinctive, gravelly tone, *"Life would be meaningless without my Rita. I depend on that woman more than she could ever imagine. Hell, at my age, it'd be suicidal to leave port without my medical officer. Pretty damn boring, too. That lady has a knack for keeping my life interesting."*

"Lacey, could we get another round?" Rita said, drawing Lacey's eyes from the *Local on the 8s*.

"Sure thing, darlin'. I'll be right there," she said, while waiting to see the local radar. Autumn weather patterns on the island often include pop-up thunderstorms that flood the streets near the waterfront before rapidly surrendering to the return of bright sunshine, only adding to the already stifling humidity. Not seeing even a blip of bad weather on the radar, Lacey grabbed the rum to prepare their drinks.

Gently nudging Rita, Gus said, "Aren't you going to ask her? You know, what we talked about last night."

"I remember! — Lacey, Gus and I were thinking you should come with us this year. You've always said you would one of these days. Our first stop just might be Cuba."

"I wish I could, but I can't. My passport has surely expired by now, anyway."

"No need to worry about that," Gus said. "I told you before, you don't need a passport the way I navigate. As long as we keep a few extra hundred dollar bills on hand in case anyone would need convincing. Pack a bag, grab your cash and come along."

Welcoming to the point of being parental, without the typical restrictions associated with responsible parenting, Rita and Gus expressed enormous compassion for those within their flock. Whether on a day sail or an extended journey, they made everyone feel at home aboard the Gypsy Rose.

"That'd be wonderful," Lacey said, serving their drinks. "I just don't see how I could pull everything together in time."

"That's a lame-ass excuse," Gus said.

"Really, you guys. With things in my life the way they are right now, I'd be leaving too many loose-ends behind."

"Speaking of loose-ends," Rita said, "what's your boy Roger have to say about this new friend of yours?"

"What on earth are you talking about?"

"Now, Lacey. Don't go giving me that innocent act. You know exactly who I'm talking about. The new guy you've been flirting with all week." Turning to Gus she said, "You said his name's Blake, right?"

"Look at that face, will you? The girl's blushing," Gus said. "You've sure got some explaining to do. Didn't your daddy ever tell you a girl should dump one guy before taking up with the next?"

"Now, Gus. You be nice to her."

"It's okay, Rita. After all these years, I've gotten used to his smart-ass comments. Now if you'll excuse me, I'd better check on the rest of my customers."

Once Lacey was out of earshot, Gus said, "Rita, I betcha that man doesn't have a clue what he's messing with. He seemed like a smart fellow. Let's hope he's smart enough to keep himself out of trouble."

"I'm not so sure it's troubled. Have you ever seen her so taken by a guy?"

"No, I haven't, but he still has the Detective to contend with. Roger may be a good guy and all, but he's still a cop and probably not above using his authority creatively. Blake could end up screwed in this town if he pisses off Morales."

"Morales has seemed a little tightly wound these days. But I can't imagine him ever doing something—"

"Come on, Rita. He's a man, and a Morales. Neither of which are known for their outstanding decision-making abilities."

"Now, Gus."

"Seriously, Lacey's one hell of a catch. No way is Roger ever going to give her up without a fight. At least, I know I wouldn't."

"Shush, you dirty old geezer. Here she comes."

"What are you two whispering about over here?" Lacey asked, making her way back behind the bar.

"Just talking about you," Gus said.

"Are you two still discussing my love life? Well, I could use a bit of advice if you promise to keep it a secret."

"You know your secrets are safe with us," Rita said.

"Then we were right," Gus said. "The new guy's caught your eye."

"I should have known better from the start, but things aren't working with Roger. I've felt trapped ever since we started dating. After spending only one night out with Doc, I realized how much Roger doesn't get me."

"Damn, girl! You don't waste any time," Gus said. "You've already spent the night with him?"

"Quiet down, you dog," Rita said, "and turn up your hearing aid. Not spent the night. She said a night out. You're missing the whole point."

"Are you kidding me? I'm not missing a damn thing. Mark my words, you two. Once Morales catches wind of this, he'll run that man's ass off the island."

"I'm sorry, Lacey. You're going to need to ignore him. He's been in one of his feisty moods all day."

Warning Gus to keep quiet by giving him the evil eye, Rita pushed ahead, thirsty for the scoop. "This new friend of yours, catch me up, darlin', while you fix us another round."

Lacey lowered her voice. "Doc is a different sort. He's fun, smart and hopefully genuine. Accomplished, too. A rare find around here. Whatever it is he did for a living, it took him all over the world. You know, after dating a totally safe and predictable guy, I've got to admit, Doc's intrigue makes me hot."

"When do I get to meet this man?" Rita said.

"Soon. I'm surprised he hasn't come in yet. I'd think he'd remember I'm covering for Smythers today."

"So, tell us about your date. I want every little detail."

"It was last night. We went sailing at sunset, had dinner at Pepe's, closed Virgilio's after dancing all night, and then he walked me home. And before you ask, Gus, nothing happened once we got back to my place."

Showing his kinder side, Gus said, "Sounds to me like you've hooked a prize catch. If anyone deserves a good man, it's you. A little advice, reel him in slowly. The lively ones can be hard to handle."

.18

"I told you we should've taken my truck," Kendra said the moment Oswald ended his call with the Mercedes Benz dealership back in Milwaukee.

"And I told you to drop it. That little self-righteous attitude of yours isn't making matters any better. How could I have known my car was going to die on us?"

"What'd they say?"

"Their automobile hauler is out on other calls, so we shouldn't expect anyone to arrive for at least a couple hours."

"Are you shitting me?"

"Worse still, we may be spending the night in Milwaukee. The agent mentioned the replacement parts would likely have to be overnighted from Chicago. I'm sorry, Kendra. This was the last thing we needed today."

After several deep breaths, she said, "You know what they say: shit happens."

Oswald smiled in appreciation of her willingness to take him and his Mercedes Benz off the chopping block. He ran his hands over the top of his balding head as to wipe away the tension. "We've got time to kill. What do you say we take a stroll back to the last exit? Who knows? Perhaps there'll be a Starbucks waiting for you there."

"And on the way, you'll tell me about my PAS profile."

"I'll tell you as much as I know."

"See, I knew you'd eventually give in, and I sure as hell didn't need your psychological profile to tell me that."

Walking against the flow of traffic, combating the harsh roar and blustery winds generated by the passing semis, Oswald deliberated on just how much of Kendra's hidden psyche to reveal.

"Gittinger postulated that each person is born with an innate collective of traits, talents and, of course, deficits. This *primitive* personality type, as he termed it, is manifest in the individual's intellectual, procedural and socio-interpersonal styles. Their distinct combination of inborn components, for better or worse."

"Okay, but what am I?"

"I'm getting to it. You must first grasp the basics for this to make sense."

"If that's the case, you're not doing a very good job."

"Be patient, I told you this is not my area of expertise. If I may continue, the PAS utilizes three polar, or opposite, descriptors to define a person's cognitive makeup. A subject is classified as either Internalized or Externalized, Regulated or Flexible, and Role Adaptive or Role Uniform. It's the interaction of these three domains that defines his or her unique personality."

"I'd be a hell of a lot better off if I could be taking notes," she said.

"I find it helpful to use the abbreviations—I/E, R/F, and A/ U."

"I'm listening."

"The first descriptor, the I/E dimension, defines a person's intellectual style. More simply stated, where the mind's attention is focused. The I individual will be primarily drawn to the world created within the mind, whereas the E personality type tends to be preoccupied by the world that exists outside the mind."

"Alright. I'm getting it."

"In the purest, most extreme sense, traits associated with the I personality include shyness, narcissism, flat affect, passivity, reclusiveness, and a inability to form meaningful relationships."

"I sure as hell hope I'm an E."

The outgoing E, on the other hand, is dependent on their environment, even to the extreme of an inability to function if deprived of external stimulation for too long a period of time. For the pure E, silence is anything but golden."

"Hey, the E definitely sounds like me."

"There's a lot more to it than that, Kendra. Allow me to continue. The second dimension is the R/F continuum. From the point of birth, a person is either procedurally Regulated or Flexible. The R individual is orderly and detail-oriented. The extreme R is rigid, insensitive and stubbornly logic-tight in their thinking. Now its opposite, the F personality, is discernible by their elevated level of sensitivity and intuitiveness. These individuals also have a high tolerance for ambiguity and they tend to learn best by trial and error. However, in the extreme, the F individual can be emotionally dysfunctional and chaotic."

"Both of those kinda sound like me, and not in a very good way."

"Generally, all individuals are a combination of both extremes, on all of the dimensions. Moreover, the PAS is a developmental model of personality, thus it looks at how attributes of one's style vary over the lifespan. I'll explain more about that in a moment."

"Something you can explain to me right now is, how far back is that last exit? Coffee goes right through me. I might need to hit the bushes if we don't get there soon."

"It can't be that much further. Now pay attention. I'm almost finished with this part. Finally, on the last dimension, a person is defined as Role Adaptive or Role Uniform. This variable describes how a subject perceives social cues and how they relate to others."

"Let me guess, the A one is the good one."

"The qualities associated with the A personality type are celebrated to a greater degree than their U counterpart. The A personality is differentiated from the U in that the Role Adaptive individual is more spontaneous, socially apt, engaging, and appropriate in response than their opposite, the U."

"I am so definitely an A. As A as they come," she said. "I can hold court in a room full of men better than any woman I know. If given even the slightest glimmer of hope of bedding me, they'll say or do anything. Like a deer in the headlights, just waiting to be run down."

Oswald anticipated this moment, the point when Kendra would have to face her lies to herself. Not uncommon, even the most insightful of subjects tend to misinterpret their psychological self. An emotional safety net that protects one from the painful pitfalls of past hurts or current shortcomings. At this point, protecting Kendra from the realities of her psyche was not an option. There was no turning back. The truth was likely what Kendra needed to discover.

With tough love engaged, Oswald responded. "Truth is, Kendra, you're not an A. Actually, something more along the lines of a heavily uncompensated U. One should be careful not to confuse the expression of intense sexuality and an appealing style with adaptability and social awareness."

"Uncompensated? What's that mean? Whatever it is, you sure as hell don't make it sound like it's a very good thing."

"The concept of compensation or, as in your case, the lack of it, leads us into the intricacies of Gittinger's methodology. As I mentioned earlier, the PAS is a developmental model of personality, which takes into consideration the impact environmental factors had in molding the individual. From the point of birth, a person's inherent predisposition, their primitive personality type, is continually manipulated through interaction with one's exclusive set of life experiences. This, in turn, dictates the maturing individual's adult personality, their unique set of temperaments and styles, as well as his or her distinctive blend of neuroses and eccentricities."

"You're saying we're born into this world as who we truly are, but once our parents get their hands on us, we're essentially destined to be totally and *uncompensatingly* screwed-up for life."

"There is an element of truth to that, however, hopefully where we begin this life is not where we end up as an adult. If that were the case, our world would be inhabited by hordes of self-interested and somewhat psychotic animals. If not for the process Gittinger calls compensation, or what you refer to as our parents getting their hands on us, the individual would become crudely satisfied, yet not well equipped to integrate into society as a whole."

"You're saying that being uncompensated is a bad thing, right?"

"I really don't know the PAS to such a degree that I could properly respond to that question. What I do know is, your profile indicated that you would make an excellent analyst and field agent for Midwest Operations. That's precisely what I got, an exemplary stateside employee."

"Only stateside? I'm not good enough for international placements?"

"You've always been so hard on yourself, but I have never seen you so fragile. I guess I hadn't realized how emotionally dependent on Jake you'd become."

Hearing that painful truth, Kendra snapped. "Fragile! What the hell are you trying to say? I don't need him." Her voice cracking as she raged. "Screw this! I'm not holding it any longer. I've gotta pee!"

Kendra, unable to conceal the tears that escaped to stream down her cheeks, ran down the embankment to a clump of weeds to find relief. Pulling herself together, as she pulled up her panties, she wiped her telling red eyes and rejoined Oswald at the expressway's edge.

"Perhaps right now isn't the best time to delve so deeply into the inner-workings of your mind," Oswald said. "We have enough on our shoulders to deal with as it is."

"No. Give it to me straight. Jake told me I'm on the verge of a life changing epiphany. He believed each of us is put on this earth with gifts that we're to share, which will ultimately lead us to discover our purpose in this life."

"Jake said that? I never picked up on the philosopher in him. I wonder why he never shared that side of himself with me?"

"I'm sure it was nothing personal. Jake keeps his cover pretty damn tight," she said. "And you're right, I could use a break from all this psychobabble."

"Good idea," he said, needing to internalize for a while. "Lord knows I could certainly use a few moments of silence."

"Oswald, do you believe there's any chance Jake will come back with us?"

"We can only hope. In case he doesn't, it would be judicious for both of us to begin drafting a Plan B."

"Plan B?" she said sadly. "Maybe I'll just come along with you on your Plan B. I've really got nowhere else to go."

.19

With a rap upon her wood-framed screen door, interrupting the angelic song of her wind chimes, and too, her daydreams of Blake, Lacey softly called out, "Hey, sailor man."

"Sailor man?"

The tenor that replied was not the vibrato of the one she had so anxiously been anticipating.

"Oh hey, Roger. Come on in."

"Oh hey, Roger? What's that supposed to mean?"

"It means, hi and you're welcome to come in," Lacey mocked, approaching the doorway to flip open the eye and hook latch.

"You were expecting someone else. I mean, what's with the sailor man comment? You've never called me sailor man before."

"I guess you must be right, Roger. I don't believe I have called you sailor man before. So, are you coming in or not?"

Still positioned on opposing sides of the doorway, Lacey watched as the veins in Roger's neck began to bulge.

"I don't know if I'm coming in or not. You haven't answered my question. What's with sailor man?"

"Really, Roger? It's come to this? We're actually standing here fighting about the way I greeted you? Excuse me, but I've had that damn song stuck in my head all day."

"What song?"

"Does it really matter?"

"Well, maybe it does matter to me. Obviously, it doesn't really matter to you!"

"The Popeye song! I've had Popeye the Sailor Man stuck in my head all flippin' day. Is that an acceptable answer, Detective?"

She twisted from the doorway and retreated to her futon to regroup, pulling Sinatra to her lap for moral support. Roger had never been one to show up unannounced. He was a true gentleman in that regard. Until now. Lacey assumed he had intentionally made a surprise visit to catch her at her game, or at the very least, catch her off-guard.

"You failed to answer the other question," he said.

"Will you please stop, already? Don't even treat me like some criminal you just apprehended."

"You sure are acting like one, intent on avoiding my questions."

"You are, you're actually interrogating me. Worse, you don't even see it. I'm not letting you in my house with that attitude, mister. I thought we were friends," Lacey said, quickly realizing the deficiency of her words.

"We're friends, alright, Lacey." Wired, he began to pace. "So, were you?"

"What?"

"Expecting somebody else?"

Keeping Sinatra held tightly in her arms, Lacey returned to the door, unsure if she should slam it in his face or give him another chance. "No, I wasn't expecting anybody. Before you showed up,

I was looking forward to having a civil conversation with you over dinner tonight. You've done a damn good job of shooting down that hope."

"Great! Now, this is all my fault. I came over here to have a mature conversation with you. Not this ridiculous cartoon craziness you roped me into."

"Roger, I'm not even going to ask you to explain how I caused this."

"Is he on his way over?"

"You're totally flipping out, Roger."

"I wouldn't have been surprised if I'd found him here. That's right, admit it. You were thinking about your date with that guy sailing on my boat."

"If I can't spend time with a friend without you going off the deep end—"

"It's that stranger you call a friend. I don't trust him."

"Wrong, Roger. You don't even know him. The fact is, you don't trust me." Turning away, speaking just loudly enough for Roger to overhear, she said, "Fine. I guess this means I'm not buying him dinner."

"That's right, Lacey. You don't have to spend your money on me ever again. Better yet, it's over! You don't have to deal with me ever again, you—you."

"Yes, Roger? Me, what?"

"You, nothing! But be sure to tell that new boyfriend of yours to watch his back in my town. One slip-up and I'll be all over his ass," Roger said, retreating from the object of his fury.

20

MONDAY | 20 OCTOBER | 18:34 EST
Latitude = 24.5608, Longitude = −81.8073
Zero Duval Street, Hot Tin Roof at Sunset Pier
Key West, Florida

Kayaking the day away provided the ideal venue for evaluating the new life I had engineered for myself. From my analysis, Blake's world had measured up to my expectations rather nicely. The freedom it afforded was as I had always imagined it would be. Oddly, while in such a place of serene contentment, I clumsily permitted a few dark shadows from Jake's world to penetrate my paradise. Drifting between the salt ponds and the sea, in the straits of humble appreciation, I was forced to revisit my angst.

Responding to the alien names I was required to regularly change, while too, keeping my stories straight, had never been an issue for me. All in a day's work for a government operative. The challenge I faced was the ability to be honest with myself, or for that matter, anyone else.

Slowly paddling through the dense mangroves in the suffocatingly brutal afternoon heat, I decided today was the day to test the turbulent waters of truth. I was finally going to come clean. Only not with Lacey. That would be far too risky. However, Kelley appeared to meet all the necessary qualifications to serve as the guinea pig for trying out my latest shtick—being real.

Upon returning to my lair, sandy, salty and sweaty from my adventure on the slow seas, I informed Kelley to freshen up and put on his Sunday's best. That is if he'd like to join me on my second visit to Hot Tin Roof since arriving on the island. The food was, as expected, superb. The wine selection, impressive. The ocean view offered to sunset diners, unmatched. Yet the single element that so quickly drew me back to this elegant eatery, hosting a sugar plantation feel, was the genuine island-style warmth and lighthearted hospitality.

Arriving at the restaurant, I suggested to my dinner partner, who emanated a distinct *Eau de Old Spice*, that we dine at the bar. Mostly for the quick response time for obtaining a fresh cocktail, but too, for the distraction of the bartender. When men dine together, a woman behind the bar establishes a masculine comfort zone. A focal point for a man's wandering eye. Beautiful and buoyant, our bartender Sheila was not only a delightful distraction, she exhibited a performance artist's skillfulness at the craft of martini preparation and presentation.

"Seriously, Kelley, you can tell a lot about a person from the most innocuous of events, if you simply pay attention to their markers," I said, being rudely interrupted by a frantic and swirling ringtone set to maximum volume. Along with just about everyone else in the place, I glared across the room to identify the culprit—a spindly, evenly tanned and Tiffany's sterling silver-adorned brunette who needed to be informed that it is proper decorum to turn one's phone to vibrate when dining at such an establishment.

"Markers?" Kelley asked.

"Yes, a person's most basic and often overlooked expressions of individuality. Once tipped off by a marker, other characteristics associated with that individual can be accurately defined."

"I'm not sure what you mean," he said.

"Take our noisy lady friend, the one with the obnoxious ringtone. Using her chosen phone melody as a marker, we can precisely assemble detailed assumptions on a variety of other aspects of her life."

"That's utterly fascinating."

"Let's try this," I said. "Take another look at her and tell me what you see, keeping in mind her ringtone."

He casually turned for a quick visual study of our target.

"I believe I'm fairly gifted at reading people. God knows, at my age, I should be," he said, beginning his appraisal. "Attractive woman, though she's more than a little anorexic, and rather hyperactive."

"Definitely. That's good, Kelley. Now, give me specifics on her lifestyle choices—husband, kids, career. Things of that nature."

"Let me see." Kelley paused to finish off his extra dirty and dry vodka martini. "To start with, she is obviously a tourist. They're the only ones you would see wearing that much jewelry on this island, not to mention, that expensive of jewelry."

"Quite astute, Dr. Kelley. Keep going with it. What else can you reveal about our suspect's world?"

"I'd say she's a school teacher and mother of two, lives in one of the New England states, or maybe Jersey, and is married to a professional. A doctor or an attorney, or some other professional along those lines."

"You should have stopped at noting she's a tourist."

"Pray tell, was I that far off base?" He quivered. "Just how far?"

"Far. Very far." I took my final sip and captured Sheila's attention to order another round.

Assuring she would perform her duties properly, Sheila repeated our order. "Bombay, a little dirty for you, Blake and a Kettle One, extra dirty and extra dry for you, Kelley."

"That's perfect," I said. "Thank you, Sheila."

Kelley continued. "Please, master, enlighten me."

"Using her marker, I'm now able to confidently assess that this Caucasian female, 40 to 45 years of age, is a U.S. citizen, and native to one of the southeastern states. She has been divorced for at least five years and has one child by her ex-husband. Hopefully it's a male child. If so, then he lives with the father."

"All that from just her ringtone," Kelley said.

"Shall I continue?"

"Of course, but how about something scandalous," he said, sliding his empty glass out of the way in anticipation of our next round.

Nibbling on the remaining gin-soaked olive from my martini, I said, "I bet she talks a mile a minute. If she works outside the home, odds are she's a realtor. Commercial property, I would gather. Oh, and too, she's likely a gold digger. Not to the level of prestige that you had suggested, a doctor or lawyer. She's probably living with the man whom she had the affair that ended her marriage. The only reason she isn't married to her new man is that he's apparently intelligent enough not to risk half his fortune on a woman known to cheat."

"Good material, Blake. That's an intriguing game, but how could we possibly know that your impressions are accurate, and mine are not?"

"Here comes our opportunity to find out," I said, noticing our target headed our way, presumably looking for the restroom. "Sit back, relax and watch me pull this one out of my derrière, my fine fellow."

"I'm ready for the show," Kelley said, not aware that Sheila wasn't missing a bit of the act, either.

"Excuse me, Miss. Are you looking for the lavatory?"

"Well, yes I am. Thank you, sugar. Lord knows, a girl's got to powder her nose," she said in a syrupy southern drawl set to fast-forward.

"The restroom's are down the hallway at the far end of the dining room," I said, aided by hand gestures. "Say, haven't we met? I'm sure we have. You and your, what is it, Steve?"

"No," she said with a look of surprise. "Steve is his brother. Stu's my husband's name. My ex-husband. We've been divorced going on eight years now. I take it we must have met in Asheville."

"It was Asheville. That's been a lot of years ago. But I would never forget such a delightful and beautiful lady," I said, taking her hand in dramatized kindness, laying it on extra thick. "So, let me reintroduce myself. It's Blake."

"I'm Cathy." She graciously, yet hurriedly shook my hand as a means of making me let go of hers.

"So nice to see you again, Cathy. Oh, and excuse me for being so rude. This is my associate Kelley. We're down here looking at a few commercial real estate opportunities."

She smiled at Kelley politely before giving us the sales pitch. "How ironic. That's my business. Well, not here in Key West, but back home. I'm a commercial broker in Atlanta. Here," she scrambled through her now retro-stylish Coach bag to find a business card, "if y'all find yourselves looking for investment opportunities in Atlanta, I'm your gal."

"Good ole Hotlanta, you say. I haven't visited there for quite some time, other than connecting through Hartsfield. But I do have fond memories of many a southern night spent partying it up in Buckhead, back in the day."

"We truly enjoy living there. So much to do, and you'll find that our economy has remained remarkably stable. It could be well worth your while to call me."

"How ever did you end up in Atlanta?"

"We relocated there shortly after the divorce became final. By we, I mean me and my wonderful man friend. That's Larry over there." She directed, flamboyantly waving to a Tommy Bahama wearing and gold chain sporting gentleman until he caught on, returning a smile and wave hello. "He owns a chain of boat dealerships throughout the Southeast. Not bad for an old country boy."

"Or country girl," I said. Thankful she didn't get it. "And your son? How is he?"

"Stu Jr. How sweet of you to remember him. He's doing just fine. He doesn't live with us in Georgia. His father and I decided it'd be best if he stayed in Asheville after the split. Stu's a big high school senior. He'll be going off to Knoxville next year to attend community college. We're all sure proud of that boy."

"As you should be." I said, as if I really knew. "Cathy, I won't hold you up any longer. It was certainly a pleasure seeing you again. I've got your card should we consider doing business in your neck of the woods."

"What a coincidence running into you all the way down here. It's a small world."

"Please, send my best to Stu."

"He'll be so surprised. In Key West of all places," she said with far too much enthusiasm. "And Kelley, it was truly a pleasure," she said before scurrying off to the powder room.

"Brilliant. Simply brilliant," Kelley said. "You collared her from head to toe. You must explain."

"I will. Before we go there, how about we order dinner?"

21

MONDAY | 20 OCTOBER | 19:41 EST
Latitude = 24.5573, Longitude = -81.7995
Lacey's Cottage on Love Lane
Key West, Florida

H*ello. You have reached the voice mailbox of Detective Roger Morales of the Key West Police Department. I am not available to take your call at this time. Leave a message at the tone and I will get back to you at my earliest convenience. If your call is regarding an actual emergency, immediately hang up and dial 911. Thank you, and have a safe day.*

Listening to his words with fresh eyes, Lacey noticed Roger's almost mechanical manner of speaking.

"Hi, Roger. It's Lacey. Not taking my calls this evening? I tried you a little bit ago, but you probably already knew that. I guess I'll leave a message this time. Wow, that was some fight this afternoon. I think you'd agree, totally ridiculous on both our parts. So, from my end, please accept my apology. I didn't mean to push your buttons. That's the last thing I intended to do, but I did."

Roger's silent treatment, by means of avoiding her calls, had attained its intended outcome. Lacey was feeling his pain.

"I know you've been having doubts about us. I'm not real good at relationships, anyway. What I'm trying to say is, I know it must be difficult to date me." Lacey paused briefly before speaking those words. "Even if our relationship has run its course, we don't have to let that stop us from remaining friends. And Rog, I feel terrible about how things have turned out between us. We need to talk, at least I do. Please, call me."

Pressing the End button while looking to capture Sinatra for sympathy, Lacey reflected on the rapid self-destruction of their relationship. Choosing to live her life in a lie, each step she took grew more complicated. Under such circumstances, finding true love without truth, impossible.

.22

"You absolutely must tell how you do it." Kelley said the moment Sheila had finished taking our dinner order.

"Do you mind waiting until I put your order in? I'd like to hear this, too," Sheila said, exposing that she had been eavesdropping. "You understand, I couldn't help but to overhear, and I've always considered listening an essential part of my job."

"You're quite good at your job," I said. "So good, you really must prepare us another round of those delicious martinis."

"Another round it is. This time, they're on me."

"Alright, here's the deal," I said. "The decisions we make in life determine who we are, while also defining what we perceive as appealing or desirable. With our friend Cathy, her ringtone is an audible expression of her personality, what she feels is representative of her lot in life. Applying that small piece of insight to our subject, we can begin to predict other aspects of her behavior and her world. Now Sheila, it's your turn. What else does that ringtone says about our victim?"

"She's jittery, and that volume level. In a restaurant? Definitely zero class."

Kelley followed with his perspective. "More inline with a chaotic mess, as in, her life must be in shambles."

"See, you two get it. Now moving forward, every new detail we obtain about our asset must be viewed through the prism of our initial premise, what we refer to as a marker."

"I see what you're saying," Kelley said. "However, that's a long way from you knowing her ex-husband's name."

Sheila chimed in. "Wait a minute. You said his name was Steve, which happened to be her ex-brother-in-law's name."

"A lucky, yet calculated guess. If we were in a Latin American country I may have guessed Eduardo or Carlos. Either way, I knew she would correct me. There's nothing magical about it. We can learn so much about others by simply paying attention. That, and, coming from a man who hits his mark 90% of the time, it takes raw talent to succeed at this game."

"You're that good, huh?" Kelley asked.

"Undoubtably, but that other 10% can sure come back to haunt you."

After a long and careful first sip of his fresh martini, Kelley said, "Walk us through it. For example, how ever did you come up with Asheville?"

"I didn't, she offered it to me. Only because I led her to the point of believing we had previously met."

"She and her ex will be racking their brains to figure out who in the hell you are," Sheila said.

"It's a fun game," I said, as one who appreciates the many possible outcomes in life's seemingly arbitrary chain of events. "Here's how I did it. When her cell phone began its annoying performance, their server was pouring a refill of her drink. I'd noticed, just prior to that event, he had asked you, Sheila, *Which is the sweet tea?*"

"Right, I remember that."

"That event, in and of itself, alerted me to other potential qualities of our target. Being a sweet tea drinker, I could comfortably assume she is Southern born and raised."

"That's simple enough," Sheila said.

"A potentially more telling indicator I interpreted from her drink of choice is, Cathy's likely either a recovering alcoholic, or on some serious antidepressants that don't mix well with alcohol. I mean, she's an obvious party girl, or was. Excuse the social profiling, but I noted at least three tattoos on various body parts. Indicators that are not typically found among church ladies or civic leaders."

"Impressive," Kelley said.

"Now, my speculation on her career choice was intuitively calculated by drawing on my years of experience. I'll explain. Again, our marker, her frantic ringtone set to high comes into play. If you recall, I said if she had a career, it would likely be real estate related. That's based on my assumption that she doesn't work out of an office. None of her colleagues would long tolerate her ringtone. Too, that chaotic tone is fitting for the career choice of one who tends to thrive on fast-paced and short-term business interactions. Real estate was simply a good call on my part. She could have just as easily been in advertising sales or perhaps a manufacturer sales rep."

"You are good," Sheila said.

"Well then, get ready for the juicier side of her life," I said, taking time to catch-up on a couple sips of my martini.

"Then there's the gold digger aspect of our sterling silver-wearing harlot. Excessive fashion statements are one undeniable indicator of a kept woman, yet the perfect tan sealed the deal. Since she doesn't like to work much, I inferred that would include the labor of caring for a child. So, as I said before, if she and the ex had a kid, hopefully it's a boy. Southern men are far better prepared to raise a son than a daughter. And finally, for such a jewelry-wearing princess, the noticeable lack of an engagement ring or wedding band suggests her gentleman friend is a damn good businessman, not willing to risk losing his fortune to the mysterious ways of a woman."

Mesmerized, Kelley said, "You had her to the point she was willing to tell you anything. All you had to do was ask."

"That's the way it works. I provided enough detail to establish trust. Then, to obtain additional information, I merely preyed on the predictability of human nature. People want to connect, and they want to believe."

"Well done," Sheila said as she made room on the bar for our appetizers. "You set her up and she filled in the remaining blanks—like names, locations and even contact information."

"Exactly," I said. "I don't mean to make her out to be a terrible individual. Sitting here, dissecting her life, we were bound to find the dirt. We usually find exactly what we're looking for. Cathy's likely no worse or no better than any of us."

"People who live in glass houses shouldn't throw stones," Kelley said with a mouth full of crab cakes.

"True, and, let him who is without sin throw the first stone," I said, "and from what I've seen, everyone on this island is merely a stone's throw away."

"You figured us out pretty quickly," Sheila said.

Kelley, again with a full mouth, said. "How ever did you develop such an intriguing talent?"

"All part of the skill-set required for my job playing a high powered sideshow fortune teller in an expensive business suit. I used to, anyway," I reminded myself, glancing down at my shorts and flip-flops.

I was confident my performance had successfully laid the groundwork to assist in substantiating the claims I would soon be making to Kelley. I figured, if I'm going to come off believable, I better reveal a few tricks of the trade. Otherwise, who in their right mind would ever believe that I'm CIA?

Finishing the last of his crab cakes, Kelley said, "Blake, I've been wanting to ask you about something."

"Sure, Kelley. What is it?"

"If you can afford dinner at a pricey place like this, why in heaven's name are you staying at that dump of a boarding house?"

"I'm glad you asked. That topic will get us into some rough territory. How about we put it on hold and enjoy our dinner? Once we've retired to the balcony for an after dinner smoke, I'll explain."

"That's fair," he said, "and thank you, Blake."

"For dinner? My pleasure."

"No, for treating me like a person."

"Why wouldn't I?"

"You know," he said, looking away in an effort to hide from his shame. "I'm nobody. I'm homeless."

MONDAY | 20 OCTOBER | 19:17 CST
Latitude = 43.1155, Longitude = -87.9173
Bayshore Inn and Suites, Brewer's Pub
Milwaukee, Wisconsin

"The front desk clerk appeared to have a difficult time figuring us out," Oswald said. "She must have thought us an odd couple to be sharing quarters."

"What'd you expect? A young hottie like me with a frumpy, old German dude."

"Or perhaps a distinguished older gentleman with an unsavory, inner-city call girl."

With the Mercedes Benz replacement part scheduled to arrive in the morning, Oswald and Kendra settled in for the night at the hotel's pub. Mustering the strength to grapple with their oversized, locally crafted ales, it was apparent their day of setbacks had taken its toll.

"I believe I've figured out what I am," Kendra said. "My personality type."

"You have?"

"It came together pretty easily. Go figure, I'm more than familiar with my shortcomings and messed-up childhood. Not to mention how those events must have negatively impacted my psychological development."

"Like all of us," Oswald compassionately said.

"I believe my primitive personality type is IRU. I'm a little iffy on the I/E, but definite on the R, and probably only thinking Role Uniform because you already informed me that I'm an uncompensated U, thank you very much."

"Internalized, Regulated, and Role Uniform. Right on the money."

"Thought so. I was a quiet, deep and super-structured kid, before I hit junior high school, that is. Then everything changed."

"And, in adulthood, your personality type has developed into what?"

"Positively Externalized, Flexible and Role Uniform."

"An EFU? That you are. Outgoing, sensitive, relating, and most alert, while being somewhat dependent on others, and awkward in unfamiliar or unplanned social situations. It's at those times you express what is a cornerstone of the EFU personality. Defensiveness."

"Defensiveness! What in the hell are you saying? I am anything but defensive."

Oswald held his tongue as Kendra directed her eyes wayward. A quick glance back at him exposed the slightly upward turning corners of Oswald's mouth, prompting Kendra to break out in exhaustion-enhanced hysterical laughter, drawing the attention of the other weary travelers in the pub.

"Lying to yourself is one thing, but doing it in the presence of someone who truly knows you is quite another," Oswald said.

"Damn that Gittinger."

"His technique doesn't leave much room for error."

"I know I'm a little oversensitive, sometimes. But when you're picked on all the time, who wouldn't be?"

"That's the curse of the U personality. U's often miss cues in social situations setting them up for cordial jabs. Hurtful, nonetheless. To avoid this, U's perfect an appropriate social routine they depend on when interacting with others."

"So, what's my social routine?"

"Why don't you tell me?" he said. "I trust you've already figured that out, as well."

"I'm afraid I have. It's all based on sexuality, isn't it? I was taught at a young age how to use sexual toying as a means of getting what I wanted."

"Keep going."

"And, I've capitalized on that personality trait to the point that I rely on it in my professional life."

"Very insightful, Kendra."

"You know, I never have completely moved beyond feeling like that hurt little girl who grew up alone in rural Kansas," she said. "That's what you meant when you said I was the right breed of agent for Midwest Operations. I don't possess the attributes needed to operate outside my comfort zone."

"Stop it, Kendra. Give yourself credit for the countless virtues you do possess. Even more, in light of how terribly that little girl was hurt in the past."

"I know you're right."

"No one is better playing the feisty, yet charming country girl. Besides, you are truly gifted at manipulating people."

"That routine's getting old. You think it's time—"

Kendra stopped mid-sentence as the waitress appeared at their table with a tray full of food and the second of their two-for-one beers. Confirming all was as ordered, the bubbly Wisconsin-blonde server smiled and sprinted along.

"You were saying?" Oswald said before attacking the dripping bacon cheeseburger grasped in his hands.

"When I was a child, my mom and I lived on the outskirts of a small community in the central part of the state. She worked at a cannery in the next town over, the same town she partied in each night after her shift. Mom was hot, so if she got too drunk to drive home, there was always someone willing to give her a lift. That meant I was left alone most of the time. That is, until I was allowed to have a boyfriend old enough to drive me the hell out of there."

"How old were you when she started leaving you home by yourself?"

"I don't know, around six or seven. Too young, regardless. With the nearest neighbors almost a mile away, there weren't other kids around."

"How'd you fill the hours?"

"I read a lot."

"How old were you when your mom began bringing her male friends around?"

"What are you trying to get out of me, Oswald?" Kendra stuffed her mouth with a massive onion ring. "I was twelve when I was first violated. I'm sure that's what led to my decreased emotional thinking and increased emotional acting out. And from the shining example set by my mom, along with the repeated sexual advances, and occasional conquests of those jerks, I learned how to handle a man. I assume it's only natural that I became desensitized to the meaningful aspects of sex."

"I'm sure that's true."

"Using the talent taught me by those assholes, I became popular with the high school guys from around the county. If those guys hadn't driven me to hate them so much, I'd probably be married to some loser, living in Backwards-assed, Kansas, with a couple of teenage brats sucking the life out of me."

"You see, good things can come out of the most dreadful of situations."

.24

Rolling thunder filled the air as Kelley and I retired to the Hot Tin Roof's balcony to relax in their oversized rocking chairs and enjoy an exquisite 1985 Fonseca Port. The sun was now hidden below the horizon, revealing a canopy of stars above. The winds rapidly cooled, coerced by an approaching storm, which forged a solemn moodiness that lingered around us as we sat and sipped and dragged in silence.

In the tranquility found this night, I struggled with the desire to align my values and actions. Confident that confession was the proper place to start, I prepared to throw caution to the prevailing winds. When the moment was right, Kelley would serve as the saint to receive my confession.

"I do say, mate, the expression on your face tells me you're a million miles away," Kelley said, breaking the silence that lasted for nearly a cigarette.

"I guess you could say that. Switzerland to be specific."

"A mental vacation can be good for the soul. I often take them to the days of a younger man, when I was still in my prime. How the world was my oyster. A far cry from my current existence."

"That reminds me. You mentioned something earlier I wanted to ask you about. You referred to yourself as nobody, because you're homeless."

"That I am."

"You may be without a roof over your head, but you sure as hell are somebody. For starters, you're my friend."

"Thank you, sir. That's very kind of you."

"And please drop the sir, will you? That routine isn't sitting well with me."

"What routine is that, sir? I mean, Blake."

"You serving as my butler. Even in fun, it insinuates a superiority over you. That just isn't right. We're all created equal members of one human family, as I recall."

"You are paying for my services."

"Just sharing what I have, my brother."

Kelley appeared relaxed, quietly content, rocking at a long, slow, rhythmic pace. Over the course of the evening, his dramatic demeanor had mellowed, giving way to a glimpse of a more confident man whose shoes he once wore.

"Blake, thank you for tonight. It reminds me of my old life in New York City."

"Except for a better climate, and from where I sit, a much more peaceful view," I said as I watched a topsail schooner being blown through the harbor.

"Definitely a better climate," Kelley said.

"Let me guess. You were a Greenwich Village boy, weren't you?"

"Oh, darling. Don't you just know it. Greenwich Village was my playground." Moving closer, Kelley lowered his voice in modest discretion. "I had a bona fide fan club of pretty boys who drooled whenever I walked into the room. They adored my accent and I was quite a handsome, young Englishman."

"I'm sure you were, old boy. And now, a debonair British gentleman."

"So kind of you." Kelley momentarily gushed before quickly drawing a more serious tone. "Now then, shall we get down to business? Isn't there something you were going to tell me?"

"You're perplexed that I can afford dinner at this place, yet live in that dump of a boarding house."

"To be quite honest, much of the behavior I've seen since meeting you perplexes me."

"Moi? Tell me," I said.

"You're a cultured gentleman, well-traveled and quite obviously, highly-educated, yet you arrived on this island acting like a wild-eyed college freshman experiencing his first taste of freedom."

"True, but is that really such strange behavior for Key West?"

"You do have a point," Kelley said. "Then what about that briefcase you chained to the sewer pipe? *Just old photo albums and family genealogy research.*"

"I wondered when you were going to ask about that."

"What are you running from, Blake? An ex-wife, the IRS or, God forbid, the law?"

"No, none of the above. What if I told you I ran out on my Uncle Sam?"

"You're military? With that hair?"

"No, not military. Chances are you're not going to believe me when I tell you."

"Oh, sure, I get it. You're a government agent, and quite possibly mad," he said. "What is the truth, Blake?"

"The truth? The truth. The truth is," I stammered as I attempted to enunciate the words I had never before spoken to one not in my sect, "I'm CIA."

"And I'm the Queen of England."

"I'm serious, Kelley. I'm a CIA operative on the run. One whose life will be considerably shorter should the Queen of England share my whereabouts with anyone."

"You're serious? CIA?"

"Serious. I'm also serious about the need for secrecy."

"Promise, not one word to anybody."

"I trust you, Kelley. Merely assuring you're aware of the gravity of my situation."

"I am now," he said. "So do tell, how in the world does one choose such a line of work?"

"No choice was given. They selected me. During my junior year in college I was contacted by the Agency and informed of my enlistment."

"How in the world did they come to select you?"

"During my initial meeting with Agency representatives I was provided documentation proving my inclusion in a longitudinal study involving a cohort of American youth, covertly tracked from birth."

"From birth?"

"Yes, from birth. A select few, those of us who exhibited the talents and disposition they sought, were notified upon turning twenty-one. With me, they didn't waste a day. The Agents appeared on my doorstep early the morning after my twenty-first birthday. At first, I figured it was a prank my friends set up to punk me while I was still in a drunken fog."

"You're serious. You really are a government agent."

"Was a government agent is a more accurate statement at this point."

"This is absolutely brilliant. I, Nolan Kelley, dining with an international spy. On the run, no less. I cannot wait to tell—"

"Kelley!"

"I know, I know. I can keep a secret. I just got excited." Kelley's flamboyance returned.

"I know you can be trusted. I've already profiled you."

"You did? Do tell."

Amused at how self-interest prevails no matter the depth of another's revelation, I said, "Quite simply, you play the role of the trusted advisor with impressive adeptness. Not many a subject exhibits your affinity for loyalty."

"Well, thank you. You sure know how to make an old gay man absolutely delighted."

"Just speaking the truth."

Kelley took that moment to relish in his goodness. A well-deserved break from the bleak contempt he typically held for himself.

"So you're a spy on the run. There must be quite the tale that goes along with your clandestine escape. *Clandestine*. That word simply reeks of mystery."

It was 11:37 p.m. on Christmas Eve. Our meeting was scheduled to begin at 11:30 p.m., sharp. In Switzerland, a country known for its rigid adherence to precision, thus an obsession with time, running even a single minute late is viewed as a thoughtless act of disregard.

Given the circumstances, my delayed arrival was overlooked. Not out of festive sentiments bestowed on this holy night. Nor out of consideration for my untimely summons to their emergency meeting, one where my attendance was mandatory. No, the margin of grace I was shown on that brisk and bleak winter's eve was not even granted out of respect for the dreadful news that lured me back to the region prematurely. Their patience was shown out of raw tolerance. I had something they wanted.

I was known as Professor Ian Mackay, an American research fellow on loan to the internationally renowned Dalle Molle Institute for Artificial Intelligence, housed on the campus of the University of Lugano, in southern Switzerland. The Institute was best known for its research efforts applying the pheromone-based communication methods of ants to such practical applications as optimizing internet traffic flow and the coordination of delivery vehicle routing.

Under the veil of such credible, commercially beneficial endeavors, other less defensible, covert experimentation was also conducted at the *Istituto*, including the initiative I had been assigned to shepherd following the untimely death of my predecessor and fellow CIA operative—an assignment that carried daunting implications for the entire world population.

Having met our project deadline, my research associates, French neurobiologist Dr. Sandrine Riviere and Swiss biochemist Dr. Giovanni Rotolo, and I took advantage of the holiday break prior to our January presentation to the Assembly. Giovanni and Sandi, having developed an intimate relationship over the course of their collaboration, were off to St. Moritz for a ski getaway. Naturally, alone, I elected for a secluded island escape to warmer climates.

My notice to return to Switzerland came via satellite phone from the Assembly's French Secretary, Émilie Chevalier. I was informed that a tragic accident had occurred on the slopes of St. Moritz and the bodies of Dr. Rotolo and Dr. Riviere had been discovered by the ski patrol earlier in the day.

Eleven hours and four airports later, I arrived at the empty parking lot of the Institute, pulling my Alpha Romero rental in the furthest spot, some forty meters from the glass and stainless steel entrance of the *Istituto*. Dragging my exhausted body from the car I popped open the trunk, my hands uncharacteristically clammy, gently removing an Esquire-sized briefcase.

The moon that hung low over Lugano eerily shimmered across the snowcapped mountains that surrounded the city. Weary from travel and the fate that awaited me, I momentarily paused, taking a deep breath to gather my wits and assume my role.

Entering Ian's passcode on the keypad, the doors of the Institute unlatched with a pronounced clap. Wrestling open the heavy glass door, an annoying truth imprisoned my soul. *This is my assigned expiration date.*

"Professor Mackay, we are grateful for your willingness to join the Assembly on such short notice, and regrettably foreshadowed by such unimaginable circumstances," Secretary Chevalier said.

"You must be devastated," Director Chen said in an emotionless, nearly sarcastic tone. "I am always fascinated by the *familia* shared among colleagues when immersed in lengthy, demanding and delicate matters. You do know what I'm saying. Don't you, Professor?"

Director Chen, a man of superior stature for his race, had led the Assembly of Nations since its creation. He was a diplomatic, yet ruthless leader who ingeniously managed the interests of the member nations. A man I never trusted, he was energized by adversity.

Taking my place at the podium, I rested my briefcase atop the table lined by the twelve most trusted consigliere of major world governments—the power brokers for a united secular world regime.

"Please accept our sincerest sympathies for the loss of your colleagues," Secretary Chevalier offered on behalf of the Assembly. "I personally want to assure you their fate was purely accidental. Since speaking with you last, I received word that the Swiss police have completed their investigation, referring to the deaths as a tragic ski accident. I'm saddened to say they noted the cause to be recklessness. Apparently, Dr. Riviere and Dr. Rotolo chose to traverse a closed trail, landing them at the rocky bottom of a fifty meter drop."

The call I received from the Secretary earlier that day was shocking and painful, but not a surprise. My colleagues and I often considered the possibility of execution as a potential consequence of our involvement in their plan.

The morning of the so-called accident, I had spoken with Giovanni, who was anything but reckless. He called to see that I was safe, questioning if I thought I was being followed. He and Sandi had crossed paths numerous times with the same two, what he described as suspicious, very athletic and sizable gentleman around the lodge and slopes. He speculated they were either body guards on holiday or hit men preparing to strike. Probably nothing to be concerned with, he concluded. Yet, obviously it presented enough concern that they wanted to check in on me.

"You do understand the urgency for our meeting, given the circumstances," Secretary Chevalier said. "With only one individual remaining who holds the results of our research, it was imperative that we proceed expeditiously. We could not risk losing the outcome of years of effort and millions of dollars. That is, if anything should happen to you."

"We are correct to assume your research is complete and the results are conclusive," the Assembly's Saudi secretary blurted out.

"Yes, gentlemen and madame. I am pleased to inform you that my colleagues, God rest their souls, and I have successfully completed our assignment. This briefcase contains the only copy of the formulas necessary to accomplish the stated goals in our charge from you, the Assembly of Nations. Once I share the documentation, you will find there are nuances to our formulas that require decoding before they may be implemented. I have elected not to include these essential components in my written report, for security reasons. Instead, the required digital key necessary to unlock our findings can only be found on this flash drive."

Reaching into the pocket of my black leather jacket to retrieve the memory card, I unveiled an expression of bewilderment as my fingers came out empty-handed. I proceeded to perform a self-imposed pat-down in an effort to locate the drive.

"Is there a problem, Professor Mackay?" Director Chen said, accentuating his concern with a rigid stare.

"There is no problem. I just remembered I placed the flash drive in the glove compartment of my rental car. Forgive me for the inconvenience. If you will excuse me for a moment, I will quickly go and retrieve it so we may proceed."

The impatient glares from the Assembly members reverberated in my head as I sprinted toward the car. Those thoughts turned to the faces of my deceased colleagues, fueling my resolve. Unlocking the Alpha Romero, I turned to take one last look at the building where I had spent most of the past six years of my life. Jumping in the driver's seat, I started the engine and began to pull away, only yielding briefly to push the red button on the remote control grasped tightly in my perspiring hand.

The massive explosion reflected in my rearview mirror indicated my personal mission had been a success. Alive, I sped away from imminent death.

"That's the way it went down, the day I became a dead man. The day after Christmas the headline across the front page of the *Corriere del Ticino*, Lugano's daily newspaper, told of the Christmas Eve explosion that rocked Lugano and destroyed a laboratory building on the campus of the University, the cause of which was still under investigation. The interesting part, the article stated no lives were lost."

"No deaths?" Kelley said. "How did they get out alive?"

"They didn't, Kelley. They were never there in the first place."

"I don't understand."

"That's the way it works in my business. The truth that is told is rarely the truth at all."

"Then what's the real truth? Did you actually kill those people?"

In that moment, I realized there is a significant obstacle to dealing with the truth—facing it.

"Yes I did. I was the one pulling the trigger for the first time in my entire career, in a profession where murder is commonplace. Certainly, there were operations where I was the one who located the target or coordinated a mission that resulted in the loss of human life. Only, never before that Christmas Eve had I been present to view the carnage of my own doing."

"You had to. They were guilty of your friends' deaths and they were going to kill you."

"Guilt can more easily be read on the faces of one's enemies than one's friends. These people were not my friends. I knew I'd never walk out of that room alive once they got their damn formula. More so, my actions were motived by an ethical dilemma."

"Ethics? In the CIA?"

"That's precisely the issue. I lived in a world of an all-consuming work culture where ethical lines were continually blurred. My post with the Agency required complete mental focus and unwavering commitment to the assignment, without regard for what was right and what was dead wrong."

"You had no other choice."

"No, I really didn't. If I hadn't acted, they would have kept destroying lives. First it was my predecessor, then my colleagues, and after disposing of me, literally millions more."

"Millions?"

"The result of our research was a process by which member nations of the Assembly could biologically modify the psychological makeup of future generations, creating a world free of conflict, and rebellion against the authorities, while at the same time removing a person's sense of passion and emotional expression."

"Now, Blake, are you pulling my leg?" Kelley asked. "Murder, international conspiracies, biological engineering? It sounds a little far fetched."

"I'm sure it does, but this type of research has been going on for decades. The difference this time, they nearly possessed the knowledge to implement such a plan. My personal ethics kicked in, perhaps for the first time in my adult life. I was to provide them with the knowledge to play God. I couldn't let that happen. — So here I am hiding out in the Conch Republic." I reached for my glass containing a last sweet sip of Port to offer a toast. "Better to be here tonight, spending a splendid evening with you, Kelley, than neatly disposed of somewhere in Switzerland."

"How in the world did you get away with it?"

"According to the official U.S. position, I was also a casualty of that terrorist attack. The reality of the situation is, the only thing that's kept me alive is the knowledge that I hold up here, under this shaggy head of hair. After returning to the States, the Agency gave me the assignment to recover and replicate as much data from our research as possible. As a result, I've been treated as a most valuable commodity."

"Why did you run? They were protecting you."

"After being shifted from safe house to safe house I finally decided I'd had enough."

"So you were willing to risk everything for freedom," Kelley said. "That I can understand. The part I don't get, why are you telling me this?"

"I need a friend. And you're the right person to place my trust. You're intelligent, loyal, way under the radar, and, well," realizing being truthful requires the full truth, I said, "the chance of anyone believing the crazy-talk of some homeless man regarding a CIA Agent on the island is rather unlikely."

"That's why you're living in a boarding house," Kelley said. "I hate to burst your pretty little bubble, Blake, but you've chosen the wrong town to keep a low profile."

"You're not the first person to tell me that. And frankly, I'm already beginning to feel the effects of it."

"Are we referring to Lacey's ties in this town?"

"That, among other concerns. I'm also a little bothered by something I did last night, a critical error in judgment while under the influence."

"Imagine that," Kelley said.

"I made a rookie's mistake. I called a friend from my last homebase to brag about the girl of my dreams I'd met down here. I didn't say where down here is, but that idiotic move could provide important leads as they commence their search. And they will come looking for me."

The thunderstorm intensified, sparked by a light show that periodically turned the dark of night into brief glimpses of a brighter day. For the first time in all my years of service, I had finally exposed the raw truth of myself to an outsider. Ranking close to treason, sharing my life experiences with Kelley was cleansing. I had long carried a private, throbbing guilt since extinguishing the threat that night in Lugano. Though the ends most assuredly justified the means, that fact didn't provide much in the way of relief for my conscience. Confessing to Kelley did.

.25

"It's a damn good thing you rolled in here," Captain Gus said as I made my way to the barstool next to his. "Lacey was about to send a search party to hunt your ass down."

"It's good to know I was missed," I said, settling in at the bar. "Gus, who's this lovely lady sitting next to you?"

"That's right. You two haven't met. This is Rita, my first mate and love of my life."

"Good morning, Rita. I'm Ja, uh, I'm Blake. It's a pleasure to make your acquaintance."

I was becoming increasingly careless with my words. Following my confession to Kelley, I awoke with an unblemished sense of autonomy. Having finally removed the CIA-implanted filter that guarded my every thought, speaking the truth came more naturally.

"Nice to finally be introduced," Rita said. "Lacey has told us all about you. That Lacey, what an angel. Any man would be lucky to catch that little darlin'."

"She is pretty amazing," I said. "Speaking of the little devil, where is she?"

"She ran off to the stockroom for another bottle of Captain Morgan," she said. "So, what happened to you yesterday? Lacey thought for sure you'd be coming in to see her."

"I took a much needed day of rest on the water. Lacey's not upset, is she?"

"If you're talking about me, you bet I'm pissed," Lacey said with a smile, hoisting a case of liquor atop the bar.

Before returning to her post behind the counter, she came over to welcome me with a hug and a kiss upon the cheek. Simultaneously, Rita jabbed Gus in the ribs alerting him to Lacey's display of affection.

"So Lacey," Gus asked, "weren't you going to tell us how your talk went with the detective?"

"You've crossed the line this time, old man," Rita said as Lacey stood quietly red-faced. "You've embarrassed the poor girl. Now say you're sorry."

"Sorry for what? Hell, Rita, in a town this small, a girl doesn't break up with a guy. He just loses his turn. Isn't that right, Lacey?"

Without finding a response, Lacey busily turned to unpack the bottles of booze.

"You might be right, Rita. Looks like I've got some makin' up to do. In my defense, Lacey's the one who brought it up, a few minutes ago."

"Not in front of her new beau."

"New beau. Is that what she's calling me?"

"I can still hear you guys." Lacey said. "Since you're all so curious, I'll just tell you. It didn't go well. What happened is he stopped by my place yesterday, unannounced. Not only did he catch me off guard, he started grilling me. So, I rebelled by pushing his buttons. That led to a ridiculous fight and now he's avoiding my calls."

"I'm sorry, Lacey. I can't help but think I've added to this drama."

"I'm a big girl. I make my own choices and can handle the fallout."

Gus butted in, "Believe me, Blake. You've added to the drama. If you ask me, I'd bet Morales is primed to kick some new-guy ass."

"That's enough out of you," Lacey said. "Another word and I'm cutting you off." Turning from Gus, she tossed down a coaster in front of me. "Sorry, Doc. I didn't ask you what you'd like to drink."

"I'm not drinking this afternoon. I just stopped by to see if you'd join me for dinner tonight."

"That'd be great."

"Say eight o'clock at Michael's? I hear they do one hell of a fondue."

"That's my favorite fancy place to eat on the island."

"Then it's a date. I'll stop by your place at a quarter of to pick you up."

"How about I meet you there?"

"Because of Roger?"

"Since he's freaking out it'd be better to play it safe."

"I don't want to instigate."

"You should give me your phone number. With Roger being all weird I'd like to have it, just in case."

"There's a problem with that. I don't have a phone."

"If you don't want me to have it, fine," she said.

"No, honest. I don't have one. I left it behind."

"Why do I have the feeling there's more to your story than you've let on? Are you married or something?"

"Married? I told you about my last relationship."

"I know what you told me, but something doesn't seem to make sense here. Everybody has a cell phone. At the very least, a pay-as-you-go from Walgreens."

"Standing here at the bar probably isn't the ideal place to have this conversation. How about we discuss that over dinner tonight?"

"I better serve up some drinks before I piss-off my customers, and Evalena."

"Then I'm going to run. Have a good afternoon."

"See you at Michael's, eight o'clock, sharp."

"No crime if you're a little late."

.26

"Thank God! Only five more miles til we hit De Pere," Kendra said. "I say we stop at Jake's apartment before making contact with Jeremy Brown. You can have a look-see for yourself and I can—"

"Freshen up?"

"Yep, and go pee."

"Somehow I already knew that, Kendra."

"At least I didn't say go piss."

Oswald quietly stared forward, preparing his delivery of bad news, purposely witheld until they had reached their destination. "You realize, if we can't procure a lead from Jeremy Brown we'll need to consider other avenues, including the utilization of Agency resources."

"That's a death sentence! Don't go getting all negative on me, Oswald."

"I'm not getting all negative. Putting my career on the line is one thing, but I have no desire to end up in a federal prison over this."

"All I ask is that we don't give up quite yet."

"I'm not so sure we have a choice. There's far too much at stake here. Need I remind you, Jake's been tagged a national security risk for a reason. If we don't find a solid lead soon, I see no other option than to notify Langley."

.27

"How I know Gus?" Kelley said. "I've done a number of odd jobs for him aboard the Gypsy Rose."

It was late in the afternoon when I arrived at La Casa Cayo to take a break before my date. Soaking up the shade on our front porch, Kelley and I sat pontificating and speculating, while watching the tourists stroll along Whitehead Street.

"Tell me, Kell. Sitting out here, do you ever feel like you're on display?"

"Somewhat similar to living in a zoo?"

"That's it. Life in the monkey cage," I said.

"There's a symbiotic relationship between us and the tourists. We entertain them and they amuse us. It seems to work out to everyone's satisfaction."

"Odd. Last week I felt like one of them. At times, a little overwhelmed by the outlandishness around here. After being welcomed into the lives of so many locals, I'm beginning to feel like one of us," I said just as our photo was snapped by a preppy twenty-something co-ed.

"I'm curious, Blake. Why all the questions about Gus and Rita?"

"My instincts tell me Gus is a trustworthy man. However, his hard drinking and gruff demeanor lead me to question my read."

"A hard life or hard living has nothing to do with one's honor. Gus, and Rita for that matter, shroud their pain in rum and jest. Nevertheless, where it counts, those two are good to a fault."

"I'm sure glad to hear that."

"You'd never know it, but Gus is loaded."

"All the time?"

"No, he's got money."

"No shit. I'd never have pegged that one."

"These winter trips he and Rita take are medical missions. Those two have adopted several port towns they visit each year providing free medical care and supplies."

"Now that's cool. I'm surprised, Lacey never mentioned it."

"She probably doesn't know. They generally don't tell anyone. I only know because I've helped load their supplies in the past."

"Covert charity. I'm impressed. So, just how loaded is he?"

.28

TUESDAY | 21 OCTOBER | 15:53 CST
Latitude = 44.4486, Longitude = -88.0606
Montagues Wine Bar, 100 South Broadway
De Pere, Wisconsin

"That's his car parked out front," Kendra said, pointing to Jeremy's rundown and rusted, maroon 1989 Mercury Grand Marquis.

"That's his? I expected Jeremy to drive something sportier, or at the very least newer."

"And you thought Critter was a piece of crap."

Their brief stop at Jake's apartment allowed time to gather their thoughts and assume their local identities. Jeremy knew the trio by the aliases Christopher and Elizabeth, and their friend and work associate from Chicago, Warren. After pushing the remote to lock his Mercedes, Warren pulled open the door of Montagues for Elizabeth to enter ahead of him.

"Happy Tuesday, my friends!" Jeremy said at the sound of the opening door. "Elizabeth! And Warren, it's been some time since you've been up this way. So, uh, what's going on? Where have you been all week, Lizzy?"

Kendra and Oswald gave each other a glance, signaling their awareness of Jeremy's awkwardness in avoiding the obvious question.

"Business meetings in Chicago," Kendra said.

"And you brought this guy back with you for a visit. It's great to see you, Warren." Jeremy reached out to shake his hand.

"A pleasure to see you as well, Jeremy."

"Have a seat anywhere you like and I'll be right with you. I got here right ahead of you. I need to check in with Paulie to see what's cooking."

Nearly falling over his own feet, Jeremy rushed off through the swinging door of the kitchen.

"He knows something," Oswald said.

"He couldn't get away from us fast enough."

"This trip just may pay off. Given his nervous reaction, I say we take the direct approach. He's not going to be able to lie convincingly."

"I agree," she said.

"You take the lead. He's obviously more familiar with you, *Lizzy*."

Jeremy returned from the kitchen with the arrival of more customers to greet. Leading them to a table, Kendra and Oswald waited patiently by the bar.

"Jeremy, I need to speak with you. It's important," Kendra said.

"It's about Christopher, isn't it?"

"Have you spoken with him?"

"No, not really."

"Jeremy, listen. You've got to tell me. Have you talked with him in the past ten days?"

"I really don't know what's going on with you two, but I don't feel right about getting in the middle of it. You know I like you, Elizabeth, but Christopher's been like a big brother to me. I've got to keep his confidence. You respect that, don't you?"

"Under normal circumstances, of course, however, our problem is far from normal. I'm serious. You've got to tell me if you've talked with Jake."

"Jake? Who in the hell is Jake?"

Growing ever more impatient, Oswald loudly intervened, without decorum or diplomacy. "That's not of your concern. I assure you, it would be in everyone's best interest if you simply comply and tell us what you know."

"Excuse me," Jeremy said, noticing they had drawn the attention of his patrons. "You're making my customers nervous, and quite honestly, me too."

"Let me handle this." Kendra said, lowering her voice to a hushed urgency. "Christopher's life is in danger."

"His life?"

"If we can't locate him, the ones that do will take him out, as in, kill him."

"Kill him, seriously?" Jeremy said in a state of shock.

"I'm serious, we need your help."

"I hope I'm doing the right thing; I know something. And Elizabeth, you're not going to like it. You two head on back to my office. I'll be there in a minute. I need to let Paulie know so he can cover for me. "

TUESDAY | 21 OCTOBER | 17:04 EST
Latitude: 24.5600, Longitude: -81.8017
Coffee Plantation, 713 Caroline Street
Key West, Florida

Settled on the wraparound porch of the Coffee Plantation, Rosalyn, with her café con leche, and Roger, his coffee black, were ready to get down to business.

"Thanks for coming on such short notice, Roz."

"I assume Miss Lacey is the reason you wanted to meet. Did you two talk?"

"We talked, alright."

"You end things?"

"Oh, believe me. It's over."

Rosalyn sipped her café waiting for Roger to take the lead. She had become accustomed to his need to muster the courage it took to bare his innermost thoughts and feelings.

"It's difficult for me to understand how I can have such strong emotions for a woman while at the same time being insanely suspicious of her. I admit I can be jealous at times, but this is different."

"Different how?"

"For one thing, she's given me reason to be suspicious. She was lying to me when I stopped by her place yesterday, or at the very least, being deceptive. Then there's the issue of the company she's been keeping."

"Sounds like good old-fashioned jealousy to me, Rog."

"No, I have reasons to be suspicious of that guy."

"Real or imagined?"

"Real. I tailed him last night."

"You did what? You've got absolutely no basis other than jealousy to spend your day off following him."

"Tell me if this doesn't raise your suspicions. I was driving down Whitehead when I spotted him sitting on the back porch of the Green Parrot. So I parked down the street, snapped a few photos of him and waited for his next move."

"I'm still waiting on the suspicious part, other than you snapping photos."

"From there, I followed him on foot. He did a couple switchbacks, constantly looking around and ending up at La Casa Cayo. No successful businessman would be staying in that rat trap. Tell me that's not suspicious."

"You've got a point about La Casa Cayo, but maybe he's broke now. We see that a lot down here."

"If he's broke, he wouldn't be eating at Hot Tin Roof."

"That place ain't cheap," Rosalyn said.

"He did, and guess who he took."

"Lacey?"

"No, thank God. But get this. He went with one of our homeless residents. A guy that hangs out at Higgs Beach in the afternoons. I've seen him around for years. Never been one of the troublemakers, though."

"I agree, not what I would have expected. Still, nothin' illegal about it."

"I'm not talking about the law, I'm talking about Lacey. Even if we're split, I've got to warn her about this low life."

"A low life that can afford fine dining," she said.

"My point exactly. My gut tells me he's likely into drug dealing or fencing stolen property. Something street-level deviant."

"You've never even met the guy. You've got no evidence of criminal activity. All your assumptions about this guy are just that—assumptions."

"Assumptions? Well, I saw Lacey kiss him at the Schooner Wharf today. That's when I called you. It was either call you or confront them, which would not have turned out pretty."

"Smart move. A confrontation between a detective and his ex's new friend would not play well in the papers."

"I know. That's why I need you to talk to her."

"Me? I don't even know her."

"That guy is bad news and she won't listen to me. I need you to tell her—"

"What? That you've been tailing them?"

"No. Maybe you say you saw him leaving La Casa Cayo?"

"Sure, make me out to be the bad cop."

"Rosalyn, you've got to help me. I know there's something up with this guy. He's not who he portrays himself to be."

"You sound like a jealous lover. But I have to admit, your instincts are usually right on."

"Then you'll do it? You'll speak to her?"

"Fine. I'll do it. Only because my partner needs to get his shit together."

"Thank you, Roz. She'll listen if you, you know, woman to woman."

"Got it, Roger. Woman to woman. That's what I'll do," Rosalyn said with a hint of sarcasm.

"What are you going to say?"

"Just let me handle it."

"Okay, but one more thing. She has my Ruger. Would you ask her for it back?"

"Give me her number, Roger."

"And see if you can find out Blake's last name. Mark my words, he's a wanted man."

.30

"Before I betray a friend, you've got to tell me what's going on. When I heard from him, it didn't sound like he was in any danger. Honestly, he sounded the happiest I've ever known him to be."

Conceding, Oswald said, "You must understand, what I'm about to tell you is a matter of national security."

"National security?"

"What that means to you is, if you should tell anyone what you're about to hear, you could be sentenced to life in prison for treason."

"Treason? Elizabeth, is this for real?"

"It's for real, Jeremy. You've gotta keep your mouth shut. Saying anything could put us all at risk."

"Not a word to anyone, promise."

Kendra began to explain. "Christopher, whose real name is Jake, is a government operative, as are Warren and I. He's been under our agency's supervision for some time, and has evidently decided to go AWOL."

"It's imperative that we locate him before our superiors find out that he's gone missing," Oswald said. "Otherwise, Jake will be in grave danger. We must know what you know."

"He left a message on my answering machine a couple of nights ago. I haven't deleted it," Jeremy said as he pulled the office phone across his desk. "I'm really sorry about this, Elizabeth. You're not going to like what you're about to hear." Jeremy scrolled through his messages until landing on the Caller ID that read: MON 01:59 AM – FL PAYPHONE. Before pushing the Play button, he said, "Apparently he's somewhere in Florida."

Jeremy, my brother. How's life in chilly Wisconsin? It's three o'clock in the morning here and I'm wearing flip-flops and shorts. I saw on the Weather Channel where you guys are going to be in the twenties tonight. I hate to rub it in, but it's in the eighties here.

Sorry to have skipped out on you without saying a word. I had the opportunity to try a new life and felt like I had to take it. Don't feel bad, I didn't even tell Elizabeth. Oh, Elizabeth. I feel like a real shit about that. Wonderful person, but as I told you before, just not what I can handle in the immediate future. Hell, I don't even know where my immediate future will be.

That brings up another matter. I've met the most amazing girl down here. Lacey, this sweet and sexy little redhead with just the right amount of spunk. Man, what a night tonight. We went sailing, drinking, dining, and dancing, and then some more drinking. I've never had so much fun. I just dropped her off at her house and now I think I need a nightcap. Can you believe it? The bars are open till four in the morning down here. Damn, I wish you could join me for one.

So, buddy, I'm going to be out of circulation for a while. I need to take this path and see where I end up. If only I could fill you in on my situation, all of this would make a little more sense. Once I find what I'm looking for, you'll be the first to know.

Oh, and Jeremy, don't say a word to anyone about this call. I'm serious, man. People will likely be nosing around up there looking for me. I don't want to be found.

The beep of the answering machine, indicating the end of the message, was followed by silence in the room. Kendra's eyes were filled with tears. Oswald reached out to her in an attempt to comfort. She pulled away.

Jeremy broke the silence. "I'm so sorry, Elizabeth. He really does care deeply for you."

"That's not of our concern at the moment." Turning to Oswald, she said, "Plenty of clues on that tape. For one thing, we have a name. I also caught what sounded like bicycle bells. Where on earth would there be bikes roaming the streets in the middle of the night?"

Jeremy jumped in, "I heard a rooster crow right before he hung up. That's kind of strange, don't you think?"

"Good call," Oswald said. "So we have a location in Florida, on the coast, where people bicycle in the middle of the night, the bars are open exceedingly late, and roosters wander the streets. It sounds more like a tropical island than someplace in the United States."

"That's it!" Kendra said. "In his apartment, right above the kitchen sink. Damn it! I should've realized."

"Realized what?" Oswald asked.

"A Zero Mile Marker shot glass. It was important to him. He said he'd had it since the 80s. That bastard, he's in Key West!"

"That's it! Good job, Kendra. We've got to get to the airport and catch the next flight out of here to Key West."

"We're not in Chicago anymore. If we depend on the commercial airline service out of Green Bay, it'll be Wednesday night before we set foot in Key West."

"What do you suggest?" Oswald asked.

"Jeremy, your friend that works for the charter service out at Austin Straubel, do you think he could arrange a flight to Key West on short notice?"

"You mean Brad. I'm all over it," Jeremy said. "Let's head out there right now and I'll call him from the road."

"Give Jeremy the key to your Mercedes, Oswald. We'll get there a lot faster if he drives."

"Yes, Kendra."

Suspicious, Jeremy said, "Oswald, Kendra and Jake, huh? So, what government agency do you work for?"

"If we told you, we'd have to kill you," Oswald said, using a worn-out cliché with a half-serious chuckle.

TUESDAY | 21 OCTOBER | 18:33 EST
Latitude = 24.5573, Longitude = -81.7995
Lacey's Cottage on Love Lane
Key West, Florida

"Detective Chapman, come in."

"Hello, Lacey. It's Rosalyn, please. Thank you for having me. I'm sure this must be awkward for both of us."

"Honestly, I'm glad to have a mediator involved," Lacey said, showing Rosalyn to a seat at the kitchen table. "Can I get you something to drink? Coffee, tea, water?"

"Got a beer?"

"Sure do. I'll join you." Lacey pulled two Coronas from a refrigerator that was covered in photographs reflecting years of Key West folly. "Roger told me you're his best friend. Quite a compliment coming from him."

"He truly is a great guy. A little crazy lately, but generally a great guy."

"Agreed, on both counts. — Cheers."

"Cheers. — I'm sure you know Roger's not the type to have somebody else do his speaking for him."

"I really throw him off balance, don't I?"

"That you do," Rosalyn said.

"I don't intend to. Our styles, they're so radically different. We're like oil and water. Like my daddy always told me, opposites may attract, they just can't live together. I'm so laid back and he's this duty-driven man who takes his responsibilities to the extreme."

"Which often comes off as being a controlling bastard," Rosalyn said.

"A goodhearted controlling bastard."

Sharing a laugh, a beer and a common concern for Roger's well-being, Lacey and Rosalyn warmed to one another. Lacey's ability to put anyone at ease immediately became apparent to Rosalyn as they chatted, comparing notes on Roger.

"I believe what Roger sees in you is something he seeks for himself."

"What's that?"

"The peace that comes with being comfortable in your own skin."

"I thought I could loosen him up. Instead, he seemed to get more and more frustrated."

"I know. That's why he sent me. You've got that boy all tangled up inside."

"You gotta let him know I'm not the enemy."

"He knows you care, and that's probably what frustrates him the most."

"I just hope we can end up being friends when this is all said and done."

"I'm sure you will. He respects you, Lacey."

Getting to the point, Lacey said, "You'd mentioned on the phone that Roger wanted to give me a heads-up. About what?"

"Your friend Blake."

Lacey rolled her eyes. "*Friend* being the operative term."

"Roger says there are discrepancies in his story."

"Discrepancies? What story?"

"To begin with, Roger said you described Blake as a successful businessman, however, that may not be the case."

"Excuse me? Has Roger been investigating Blake?"

"Not investigating. He, by fluke, found out where Blake is living."

"By fluke. Right. I'll tell you what, Roger needs to—"

"Lacey, I'm only the messenger. I agree, he was dead wrong to follow him. I've already jumped his shit for it."

"That's stalking."

"In his twisted way, he did it because he's worried about your safety. Roger has a feeling about this guy. Not that he's always on the money, but his intuition has led to many arrests."

"So what's he got on Blake that's so damning?"

"Other than his intuition, not much. There is one thing I found odd. Seems Blake is staying at La Casa Cayo, that boarding house over on Whitehead."

"Really?"

"Roger found it kinda strange a man with means would be bunking up in a place like that. Well, and too, Roger tells me he's been hanging around with a homeless guy, which could be his connection to the streets for drug dealing or moving stolen property."

Lacey thought Blake's living arrangement, coupled with the fact that he does not have a phone, was worthy of her consideration. Having a homeless friend was not. And the thought of drugs or stolen goods, ridiculous.

"I don't know, Rosalyn. Maybe he's cheap. But tell Roger I'll be sure to ask him about it," Lacey said, swigging her beer. "See. That's the problem. I can't have someone in my life that looks at everything and everyone with suspicion. He was making me crazy."

"He's concerned you're too carefree in making friends."

"Which is no longer any of his concern."

"Perhaps you both would do well to move a little toward the center. We see all kinds come through this town, girl. You've been here long enough to know that."

"I honestly don't believe Blake is some kind of criminal, and definitely not a drug dealer or anything like that."

"Would you consider giving me his last name? Roger believes he may be wanted."

"Bullshit! It's none of Roger's damn business." Lacey stood and paced the floor. "Please, tell him to back off. I was hoping he and I could move on peacefully, but right now I don't care to hear from him anytime soon."

"All he asks is that you play it safe until you've had time to get to know this guy."

"I will, but Roger needs to leave Blake alone. He's got no reason to be messing with some guy whose only crime is being my friend."

"I'm with you on that. I'll keep watch on him."

"I'd appreciate it." Lacey said.

"There is something else you should know. You said you and Blake are only friends."

"Only friends," Lacey said.

"Roger claimed he saw you two kissing at the Schooner Wharf today."

"Kissing? I gave him a friendly peck on the cheek when he arrived. How the hell would Roger know that, anyway?"

The ting of the wind chimes and purr of Sinatra filled the room as Lacey angrily bit her lip in silence. Her face turned ruddy with irritation. Not wanting to take it out on Rosalyn, she drew several deep breaths to harness her outrage.

"Rosalyn, I hope we have the opportunity to chat again, under better circumstances. If there's nothing else we have to discuss, I need time to let this sink in."

"I certainly understand, darlin'. Here, please take my card, and don't hesitate to call me if I can be of help in any way."

.32

Did you talk to her yet?

yes just left

How'd it go?

she was pissed but took ur warning

Pissed?

didnt like u stalking him

You told her?

was obvious

?

casa cayo and kiss at bar

You told her about me seeing the kiss?!

it came up

Roz!!!

dont roz me - u ask me to do ur biz for u

...

she said it was a peck on the cheek

...

Did you get my gun?

forgot

.33

"We have reached our cruising altitude. It's now safe to move about the cabin. Please keep your safety belts fastened while you are seated. We don't expect to see any bad weather this evening, so it should be a relaxing flight. You may use approved electronic devices at this time. For your convenience, PackerAir Charters offers Wi-Fi on our entire fleet of three jets. If there is anything we can do to make your flight more comfortable, please let us know. So, sit back and enjoy the flight. Next stop, Key West, Florida."

"That was extraordinarily kind of you to let Jeremy use your Mercedes while we're away."

"It's just an automobile."

"Just an automobile? You worship that car."

"It's better than having it sit in an airport parking lot racking up door dings and daily auto stowage fees."

"You have a crush on Jeremy Brown. You get all awkward when you're around him."

"No, I don't." Oswald said, his face bright red. "Do I?"

"Ozzy, you're shy! I never knew that about you."

"Admittedly, I can be somewhat uncomfortable around a desirable man."

"I knew it," Kendra said as she retrieved the laptop from her backpack that was safely stowed under the seat in front of her. "What's the name of the bed and breakfast that guy at the airport recommended? I'll book us a couple rooms."

"He wrote it down." Pulling a pink Post-it note from his pocket, Oswald said, "Here it is, the Cypress House on Caroline Street. He asked me to be sure to send his best to the innkeeper."

Kendra did an internet search, landing her on the guesthouse's homepage. "This place sounds great, and they have a free happy hour each evening."

"Need I remind you, this is no vacation."

"Just trying to make the best of a bad situation," she said.

"Jake's phone message didn't affect you like I thought it would. I'd expected you to be difficult tonight, but you haven't said a word about it."

"You mean a word about Lacey? We'll have to wait and see, but I just might kick the bitch's teeth in when I find her. Other than that, I'm fine. Enough said?"

"I see you prefer not to talk about it," Oswald said.

"She makes for an easy target to help us locate Jake. I mean, come on, how many redheads named Lacey could there be living in that small town? And by the way, who in the hell would name their kid Lacey, anyway?"

"Identifying her will be our first order of business. And Kendra, please save the teeth kicking until after we've found Jake."

.34

The garden bar at Michael's offered a relaxed elegant dining experience at one of the island's most celebrated eateries. I arrived early to assure there would be time to relax and enjoy a cocktail. Having the nervous jitters is unheard of in my field of work, however, excitedly awaiting the arrival of a new love interest is a far different matter.

Lacey would surely come expecting an answer regarding my lack of the very basics in modern communication technology, a situation that would force my hand in owning up to the truth. Yet, by the end of my pre-date beverage, I had come to the conclusion that the details of my past should be reserved for a later date. A general description of my perils would be more appropriate. A wise move, considering her association with local law enforcement.

⊕

Lacey walked through the doorway, looking as if she had spent endless hours preparing for our date. The look on her face told quite a different story. She appeared distracted and distant. I stood to greet her.

"You look absolutely gorgeous this evening," I said, leaning to embrace her, only to receive a less than expressive hug in return. "Are you okay?"

"You want the truth?"

"Is it Roger?" I asked.

"Yes, and no."

"Me?"

"I don't know."

It was clear, she was ready to start asking me questions. My glass was empty and a cocktail in hand was essential before my interrogation was to commence. I got our server's attention and ordered a round.

"Did you and Roger talk?"

"No, and apparently Roger has no desire to speak with me. He sent Detective Chapman, his partner, in his place."

"He sent a consigliere? Why?"

"To warn me about you."

"Warn you?"

"He has a feeling you're not who you say you are."

Of course my mind rushed to assume my true identity had somehow been revealed, and that Roger was quite possibly on the phone with Langley that very second making arrangements for my capture. Realizing my thoughts were overly paranoid, I pursued further information.

"What'd Roger make me out to be?"

"Your average street criminal that came down here to try his game in the tropics. A fence or drug dealer from what I understand, and possibly a wanted man."

"You don't believe him, do you?"

"I don't know what to believe. You tell me you don't have a phone, then Roger sends word that you're staying at La Casa Cayo and hanging out with street people."

"He's been tailing me?"

"I guess. To his credit, tell me it doesn't seem odd, a businessman who has no phone and rents a room in a dump."

"Sorry to disappoint you and Roger, but I'm not any of your accusations."

I couldn't say which pissed me off more, Lacey's doubts about my credibility or her ex meddling in my life. Combined, they'd put a serious damper on any hopes for a romantic evening.

"Is that all he had to say about me?"

"That was the gist of it. Do you want to give me your version of the story?"

"I'm not sure it really matters at this point. Besides, I don't know if I care to justify myself."

"I should've called and cancelled tonight," she said, "only you don't have a damn phone."

"I told you about Kendra. I left the phone so she'd know I didn't want to be contacted."

"Then explain why you stay at that boarding house."

"They offer a month-to-month rent option, which gives me time to check out places worth a long-term commitment."

"You sure have an answer for everything."

"I see. Now I'm a con artist, too."

"I wasn't saying that."

"What were you saying?"

"I don't know, Doc. Maybe this isn't such a good idea."

"You know, you're right. You should find closure with the cop before starting with someone new."

"No, not that. I meant dinner tonight. My head is really messed up after talking with Roger's partner."

"I see that."

"I'm not going to be very good company tonight," she said. "I think it's better we skip dinner."

TUESDAY | 21 OCTOBER | 22:11 EST
Latitude = 42.1879, Longitude = −87.7874
La Casa Cayo, Whitehead Street, Outside Unit A
Key West, Florida

"You're home early this evening," Kelley said, sitting on the steps of my porch, surrounded by four empty cans of Natty Ice. He lifted the last remaining unopened beer of his six pack as an offer. I held up my hand and shook my head to decline.

"It wasn't the sort of evening I'd anticipated," I said.

"What happened?"

"The ex-boyfriend is scaring her off. He seems to think I'm some sort of criminal."

"Little does he know who he's messing with. What are you going to do?"

"I don't feel like talking tonight," I said. "I'm going to sack out and get up early to spend the day at the beach, alone."

"She has you frustrated."

"This relationship already has way too much drama."

"I'm here if you need to talk."

"Thanks, Kelley." I lit one last smoke before turning in. "I could use a recommendation on which beach I should hit tomorrow."

"Fort Zach. You'll love it. It's by far the most beautiful beach on the island, and it's the most secluded, too."

"That sounds ideal."

Kelley popped open his last brew and said, "Sure you don't want my counsel? You look like you need an ear."

"No, but let's meet up tomorrow evening for a drink. By then I'll be ready to talk this through."

"Okay if I choose the bar?"

"Sure thing, Kell. You name it and I'll be there."

"My preferred place to relax in the evening is the pool bar in the rear of the Bourbon Street Pub."

"Sounds peaceful."

"That depends on your definition of peaceful. It's clothing optional."

"I believe I can handle it."

"Shall we meet at eight?"

"Works for me," I said.

"Bourbon Street is on the 700 block of Duval."

"Got it."

"I'll see you there."

.36

"It's my pleasure to welcome you to the Cypress House. I trust you rested well last night." Dave, the flamboyant and lovable innkeeper, greeted Oswald and Kendra with VIP attentiveness, having heard through the *Coconut Telegraph* of their arrival by private jet.

"Like a baby. Wouldn't you agree, Ozzy?"

"Oh, yes. My accommodations were quite comfortable, thank you." Noticing Dave's name tag, he reached out his hand to introduce himself. "I'm Oswald and this is Kendra. It's a pleasure to meet you, David."

"What brings you to our charming little island? Would it be work," Dave quickly glanced at Kendra, then slowly turned to gaze Oswald's way, "or pleasure?"

"Kendra has personal affairs to attend to, while I came along for moral support, and to soak up some sun and fun."

"I wouldn't be your best resource on the moral, but Oswald, if you would like suggestions on the fun part, I'd be happy to share some ideas. That is, if you're looking for the kind of fun us boys prefer," Dave said with a wink.

"I'd appreciate that. If you'd like, you could even show me around town one evening."

"I would love that."

"Sorry to interrupt you boys, but Dave, maybe you could help me locate a friend of a friend that lives here. I don't recall her last name, but her first name is Lacey. She's a redhead."

"The name doesn't sound familiar. Stephen, our night manager, comes in at six o'clock. He knows about everyone on this island. I'll ask him when he arrives."

"That'd be great. I can't wait to meet this woman."

"You enjoy an alternative lifestyle, as well?"

"No," Kendra said.

"Oh. — Oswald, stop in the office whenever you like and I'll give you some pointers."

"I'll do that."

"Make sure you don't miss happy hour. this evening. I'll be ringing the party bell promptly at five."

"We wouldn't miss it, now would we, Kendra?"

Dave moved on to greet the other guests enjoying their poolside breakfast while Kendra waited for Dave to get out of earshot. "Damn, his gay-dar is finely tuned. Sounds to me like you have a date."

"He was simply offering to show me around."

"No. You asked him to show you around."

"Oh, my goodness. I did, didn't I?"

"You sure did, sweetie."

"Kendra, I don't believe I can ever go back to playing straight."

"If we don't find Jake you won't have to worry about going back to that life."

"Good point," he said. "Although I believe the night manager might give us the break we're looking for."

"I don't think we should wait til tonight to begin our search. Let's split up and meet back here later."

"I'm with you on that," he said.

"Cool. You take Upper Duval Street and I'll head to Lower Duval. From what I read on the internet, Upper Duval is the artsier and gay end of Old Town. Lots of galleries, wine bars and trendy boutiques."

"So, what's Lower Duval?" Oswald asked.

"The wild, partyin' end of Old Town."

.37

As is typical of Key West, rich history is often the backdrop for a spectrum of recreation and entertainment venues. At the edge of Old Town, Fort Zachary Taylor provides just such a unique blend.

The fort, built in the mid-1800s, was erected to defend the United States' southeastern shoreline. During the Civil War era, Fort Taylor remained under Union control and was credited for its role in limiting the war by preventing Confederate supply ships from reaching their ports in the Gulf of Mexico. Today, Fort Zach is a place of celebrations and play. For me, this day, it's a place of solace.

Trying to live the lives of two people eventually proves to be disheartening. Blake's life extended a welcome breath of fresh sea air, yet leveraged its own set of challenges. What first appeared to be a spicy new reality had quickly revealed the down side of being a pretender. Fooling others was easy. Fooling Jake was not.

Jake's life, with its obvious disadvantages, allowed me to walk in familiar shoes, not that I could ever wear them again. I missed aspects of that world. Not the professional life it encompassed, but the personal relationships that were fostered there.

After last night's failed date with Lacey, I was left feeling discouraged and alone. The excitement and the hope of colliding with a potential soulmate had faded in light of her mistrust. The belief that my perfect mate actually existed had been beaten down once again. Sitting in the soft grains of sand, I doubted her genuineness, her honesty and even her potential as a friend.

My fatalistic thinking sucked the joy from my spirit, even while surrounded by the awesomeness of sand, sea and sky. Feeling quite small and lowly, I found myself thinking of Kendra, even missing her complexities and quirks. Perhaps my feelings of failure were a karmic result of the lack of concern I showed for her's, abandoning her without warning, words or, far worse, answers.

Blake's life was fun and free, yet left me feeling empty. And Jake's, painfully void. In quiet solitude I pondered, will this journey ever lead to truth, that place where I could finally find peace?

.38

Kendra strolled into the Cypress House garden minutes past the close of happy hour. Glassy-eyed from a day of searching for Jake in the island's many taverns, she spotted Oswald chatting with a group of fellow guests. Surprised by the levity of his expression, she viewed a far different man than she had previously known. Waiting for him to conclude his conversation, she caught his eye and waved him over for a debriefing on the day's findings.

"Aren't you Mr. Socialite?"

"I'll take that as a compliment," Oswald said. "I was not aware people could find me so fascinating."

"Maybe because you've finally taken that broomstick out of your ass. Since I've known you, you've always maintained complete control over everything and everyone in your world. Most of all, yourself."

"Because of my job. I had to command a level of composure befitting the position."

"Kinda sad," Kendra said.

"What's that?"

"Your job became more important than yourself."

"Just as you have done?"

Offering no response to his observation, Kendra said, "The internet had it right. Lower Duval is party central."

"Upper Duval was quite classy, if you ask me. Not blatantly gay. Although, I did notice a few establishments advertising nightly drag shows. I absolutely must catch one some evening."

"After we've found Jake," Kendra said.

"Knowing he's somewhere on this island is reassuring."

"I know. It's only a matter of time until our paths cross."

"From the looks of you, I'm not sure you would have seen him if he was standing right next to you. How much did you have to drink?"

"I didn't have that many. Just enough to fit in."

"I can't blame you. I had a few, myself."

"This town sucks you right into having fun. Even given our circumstances, I found myself becoming super relaxed. Come to think of it, I haven't even had any caffeine since breakfast."

"That's a first."

"I see why Jake chose this island for his escape," she said.

"Well, I certainly feel alive here."

"I noticed. You've sure let down your gay guard."

"What's that supposed to mean?"

"You're putting it out there."

"What's observably different about me?"

"Everything. Ever since you came out, you've been pretty damn obvious."

"I simply know I'm happy and could care less if my excitement shows."

"That's why they call it gay."

"Real cute, missy."

"Missy? Like I was saying."

"Oh, you stop it," he said.

"Whatever brought you out, I like it." Noticing Dave working his way toward them, Kendra lowered her voice. "Here comes your boyfriend."

"Kendra, please. Don't embarrass me in front of him."

"Don't you worry, lover boy."

Oswald took the lead as he approached. "Hello, David. So nice to see you again."

"You too, Oswald. I must tell you. I adore that name. Very dignified."

"How kind of you," Oswald said with a gentle touch upon Dave's shoulder.

"I spoke to Stephen about the young lady you were inquiring about, Kendra. He doesn't know her, however, he made a couple calls and was able to find out where she works. The Schooner Wharf Bar. That's just around the corner at the seaport."

"Thank you so much for your help, Dave. Ozzy, I believe I'll head right over there to say hello."

"Actually," Dave said, "I understand she works the day shift. So, you'll need to wait and catch her there tomorrow morning."

"Looks like I'll have to find something else to entertain myself with this evening," she said.

"If you enjoy live music, I would highly recommend catching the Carter Brothers at the Hog's Breath Saloon. They're a couple of Appalachian boys that play their own brand of funky and fun bluegrass. They'll have you on the floor dancing."

"That's right up my alley. Too bad our old buddy Jake isn't with us," Kendra said with a glance toward Oswald. "That sounds like a band he'd want to check out."

"Sounds like the perfect plan, Kendra."

"What about you, Oswald? What are you up to tonight?" she asked, setting the stage for the boys to make a date.

"I haven't given it any thought, but—"

Dave interrupted, "If you would like to join me this evening, I'd be delighted to show you around town."

"That would be lovely."

"I'll leave you boys alone to figure out a plan. I'm heading back to my room for a nap before the night begins."

"Then Kendra, I'll see you for breakfast at, what, eight o'clock?"

"Let's make it nine. I've got a feeling we'll both be out pretty late tonight."

WEDNESDAY | 22 OCTOBER | 20:07 EST
Latitude = 24.5529, Longitude = -81.8010
Bourbon St. Pub, 724 Duval Street
Key West, Florida

Making my way to the rear of the Bourbon Street Pub to meet Kelley at the pool bar, I found it discouraging that there was not even one beach babe in the place, just a bunch of guys. Continuing down the narrow hallway to a door prominently displaying a sign that read, *Clothing Optional: Men Only*, it hit me.

Beyond that door revealed a massive tiki bar surrounded by enormous palm trees, a rumbling waterfall that flowed into a pool of cool blue water, and lots and lots of penises. Modestly, I sought out Kelley, finding him, thank God, fully clothed at the bar.

"You found it. Come, I saved you a stool," Kelley said. "Are you all right? You look surprised. I told you this place is clothing optional."

"You told me."

"You were expecting to see some lovely ladies in the buff, I presume."

"To be quite honest, yes."

"Sorry to disappoint. Would you prefer to go elsewhere?"

"No. I'm fine with having a drink here. Just don't expect me to drop my drawers."

"I didn't expect you would. Although, a dip in the pool might help to soothe that nasty burn you got today. And since you apparently did not find your way to the shower after sunbathing, a swim would help curtail your bouquet."

"Sorry. I was running late."

I tossed my recent purchase of a disposable cell phone on the bar to validate my excuse. While waiting on the drinks Kelley had ordered, I considered the fact that a homeless man rightfully noted his concern over my personal hygiene. A lesson learned.

"We acquired a cell phone today, did we?"

"It might come in handy. You understand, me being an eligible bachelor and all."

"For Miss Lacey to reach you, or do you already have your designs on another?"

"I don't know what to do about Lacey. While at the beach today I convinced myself she's nothing but trouble."

"That didn't take long. Are your honeymoons always so brief?"

"Not necessarily, but I'm beginning to think she has more baggage than I'm ready to deal with."

"Especially since you have enough baggage for the both of you," Kelley said.

"All the more reason."

"What happened last night to ruin your date?"

"She's skeptical of me. I know telling her my story would likely resolve the issue, but to be quite honest, my gut tells me not to trust her."

"Sounds like a match made in hell," Kelley said.

"My point exactly, a no win. I feel like she's playing me, like she's hiding something. Or it could be as simple as, I have major women issues."

"Deeply rooted from childhood, perhaps?"

"No, Dr. Freud. More like the responsibilities of my job never allowed for a long term relationship."

"That sounds like a bullshit answer. When was your last long term relationship?"

"Right before coming down here, if nine months is what you consider long term. I ran out on that one, too, without even saying goodbye."

"Not an ounce of chivalry? I considered you to be more of a gentleman than that."

"I know, pretty lousy. I thought about that today, too. She really didn't deserve to be treated that way."

"No one deserves to be treated that way."

"I guess I got scared. So I ran."

"We do have serious issues with women," Kelley said.

"Not that I'm going to start hanging out here, mind you."

"What do you plan to do? Run from Lacey, then the next one and the next?"

"Running away has always worked for me, my most trusted defense mechanism," I said. "Perhaps you're right, though. Maybe I should give Lacey another chance."

"There's no need for a rush to judgement, particularly when it comes to love."

"I guess you're right."

"Besides," he said, "you need to consider, there aren't that many options available on this island. At least the ones with a relative degree of sanity."

Kelley excused himself to visit what he referred to as the powder room as I, with a newfound resolve based on the theory of supply and demand, committed to giving Lacey a second chance. I would proudly call her on my newly purchased cell phone and ask her out for a late night cocktail.

Nonchalantly glancing around the bar to see how the other side party, an eerily familiar voice resounded. Looking in that general direction, my view was blocked by the cash register. Although not an exact match, mind you, yet should Oswald Reinbold be a gay man, that voice was precisely the way he would sound. Briefly troubled by the similarity, I sipped my drink awaiting Kelley's return.

"I'm glad you're back, Kell."

"Why are you whispering?"

"Being paranoid," I said.

"Regarding?"

"I know it isn't, but the deeper voice coming from the other side of the register, take a quick glance and tell me what he looks like."

Each descriptive detail from Kelley's lips increased my level of concern. The man he saw was most certainly Oswald. Confusion gripped my mind. *Oswald isn't gay. Why on earth would he be in a gay bar sounding all gay? Could it merely be a coincidence? Could it be he's here on assignment? But no, by now he must know my status. They must have figured out where I am. Damn, I knew that phone call to Jeremy Brown would come back to screw me in the end.*

"Kelley, that's him. That means Kendra's here, too."

"Him who? And who's Kendra?"

"Oswald Reinbold, my station chief."

"With the CIA?" Kelley discreetly questioned.

"Yes, the CIA."

"And Kendra?"

"She's another CIA operative, and the woman whose heart I broke when I skipped out of town to come down here."

"You sure do know how to make life complicated, don't you?"

"Obviously. I better get out of here. Is there a back door?"

"But, of course."

"Point it out so I can plan my move."

"Behind you, around to the left. The exit takes you out to Petronia Street. To get back to our place, make a right, then a left at the next block, that's Whitehead."

"Got it. Before I go, I want to eavesdrop for a minute. I find it hard to believe that he's gay. That's not something one can easily hide from a friend."

.40

Some say the soul of Key West can be found at the Chart Room. Known as a favorite watering hole among many a local legend, from the likes of Mel Fisher, the renowned treasure hunter, to colorful Key West characters Panamah Peat, Whistle Pants and Che. Even a little known southern boy named Jimmy Buffet first played his brand of music on the island within the bounds of this infamous establishment. It's a place where grand plans had been made, lies had been told and destinies determined. Tonight was no different. On this evening, for me and Lacey, the Chart Room would play host to ours.

"You found it," Lacey said as I walked through the broad double doors of the bar.

"You were right. This place is tucked away in a garden maze."

"I'm glad you called, now that you've joined the rest of us in the Twenty-first Century."

"It's a far cry from my Blackberry, but a hell of a lot better than those filthy payphones," I said. "I could go for a beer."

Lacey called out to the bartender, "Excuse me, JJ. My friend needs a beer."

He slowly raised his head up from the newspaper he had been reading. "Sure. What can I get you?

"How about a Heineken?" I said.

"You got it, friend."

JJ slung my beer on the bar and grabbed my cash as I glanced around the tiny bar, which was no bigger than an economy hotel room. Spotting an open table, I said, "How about we take that spot in the corner?"

"Sure. A little privacy would be nice."

"You two aren't sticking around for my comedy act?" JJ joked. "I just heard a new one that's worth a listen."

"Go ahead," Lacey said. "Let us have it."

"The past, the present and the future walked into a bar." He paused and smiled. "It was tense."

After brief, polite laughter, Lacey and I made our way to our seats seconds before they would have been gobbled-up by an arriving gaggle of jovial tourists. Now safely huddled in our corner, Lacey offered me an olive branch.

"Doc, about last night. I'm sorry."

"You were having a bad day."

"And I took it out on you," she said. "I was wrong to let Roger's accusations influence my opinion of you. Whatever Roger might think, you've been nothing but a gentleman. Not only with me, with everyone."

"How about we forget last night ever happened?" I said.

"Thanks, Doc."

Knowing it wouldn't be long until Oswald and Kendra would track her down, I had to prepare Lacey for that encounter. — The time had come to offer her the truth. A version of the truth.

"On the phone, you made it sound urgent we get together tonight," Lacey said.

"I guess you could say that. It's concerning a business associate of mine. I saw him earlier tonight. Thank God, he didn't see me."

"Business associate? In Key West?"

"Yes. Oswald, my boss. Given he's here, I have to assume Kendra is too."

"Your girlfriend?"

"Ex-girlfriend," I said. "If they find me, they'll be pretty aggressive in their efforts to convince me to return."

"Why don't you just tell them you've moved on?"

"It's not that simple. I've got to be upfront with you about my past."

"Like you should have from the beginning," she said.

"Like you were with me?"

"Point taken."

"How about we both come clean tonight? If we're going to be partners in crime, we ought to know what we're getting ourselves into."

Lacey squirmed in her seat. Nervously biting her lip, she said, "I've never admitted it to anybody before. Ever."

"It's probably time you get it out. Confession is good for the soul."

"You're not a cop, are you?"

"No, I'm not a cop."

Lacey's eyes darted upward as she spoke. "It's nothing horrendous, but you go first. I need time to build up my nerve."

Accepting her offer, I began to piece together my tale from carefully selected shards of the truth. "I was a contractor of sorts, working on projects for the federal government. Ones that required a top level security clearance. Skipping out on them like I did will not be taken lightly. Now, I'm literally a man without a country."

"It's that serious?"

"Jail serious," I said.

"They'd have you arrested?"

"They're more likely to try talking sense into me and returning with them before it's too late."

"Should you?"

"There is no going back."

"You sure?" she asked. "Believe me, living on the lam is a real pain in the ass."

Lacey's eyes shot wide open in reaction to her premature admission. I let it slide.

"If I refuse to return, their only option would be to notify our agency director who would, in turn, make arrangements for my capture."

"What are you going to do?"

"Leave the island, and soon."

"And go where?"

"Out of the country is my best bet."

"You know Gus and Rita are leaving port soon."

"Exactly what I was thinking. You think Gus would consider taking me along, given my circumstances?"

"I bet they would. I'll check when I see him tomorrow."

"Thanks. There's another issue about tomorrow."

"What's that?"

"Kendra. She'll definitely come looking for you."

"Me? How would she know about me?"

"I kinda mentioned you in a voicemail I left a buddy from up in Wisconsin. He's Kendra's friend, too. I'm sure that call is how they tracked me down. If that's the case, they would also know about you."

"They won't mess with me, will they?"

"No, but they sure as hell will try to get intel out of you."

"Intel? What government agency did you work with?"

"Better that you don't know."

"How will I know who she is?"

"Knowing Kendra, she'll be obvious about it."

"Obvious how?"

"Like asking you if you're *sleeping with her boyfriend* obvious. Odds are, she won't elect to use the word *sleeping*."

"Nice. What should I tell her?"

"I left town for Miami. Kendra has an insane intuition. If she thinks you're lying, she'll drill you until she gets you to slip up. So, be careful."

"Trust me. I can pull it off."

"Thanks for doing this, Lacey. I'll make it up to you, somehow."

"There is a way you can," she said, "which brings us to my story."

"I'm listening."

Lacey fidgeted in her seat, pursing her lips numerous times before allowing a single word to escape. "At the time of my husband's death, I came to find out his business partner had been ripping us off. He had an offshore bank account in the Cayman Islands where he'd stashed a percentage of the company's earnings, as well as some of the clients' cash. After doing some poking around, I was able to get the account information. What I need is help with getting access to that money, and getting it laundered."

"What makes you think his business partner hasn't already moved those funds?"

"He's dead, too. An accident, a car accident."

"Okay. You're on the lam why?"

"The authorities think I was involved."

"Were you?"

"After my husband passed, the clients became antsy and the fraud was uncovered, so his business partner tried to pin the whole thing on me and my husband."

Somewhat believable, I considered. "Get me the details and I'll find a way to get the cash back in your hands."

"I'll make it worth your while," Lacey said.

"Nice doing business with you, partner."

We toasted.

.41

"I started without you," Kendra said as Oswald made his way to the table where she sat eating fresh fruits and breads and sipping her coffee.

"Sorry, I'm behind schedule," Oswald said. "It was quite a late night for an old boy, like me."

"I can tell by those bloodshot eyes. Good time?"

"I didn't want the night to end. I've never felt so, so—"

"Alive?"

"Desirable," he said.

"Really? You didn't drag home some island boy, now did you?"

"No. However, I did have an offer."

"Oswald, you old dog."

"It was tempting. I've never been with a man before, or for that matter, a woman."

"You're a virgin?"

"I've never had an interest in women and, to be quite honest, didn't know I could allow myself to go the other way."

"I'm glad you didn't sleep with the first Tom, Dick or Harry that came along. Nothing worse than feeling cheap the morning after."

"I did get my first kiss last night."

"That is so sweet, Ozzy. Now, what on earth am I going to get you for your sweet sixteen?"

"Stop it. I know, I'm a late bloomer."

"And quite lovable."

"Enough, Kendra. You're embarrassing me. What about you? How was your night?"

"The band was amazing, but all I could do is sit there and think about Jake."

"Today's the day we're going to find him."

"I hope so. I miss him so much."

"I'm sure you do."

"Jake being gone made me realize how much I need him."

"Don't get your hopes up. You know he's a player."

"I'm tough. I can handle whatever is to come."

Oswald began devouring his hefty breakfast as Kendra, preoccupied, poked at her fruit.

"What is it, Kendra?"

"Lacey. I'm looking forward to interrogating her ass."

"We'll go as soon as we're finished with breakfast."

"I assume you'll want to shower first, to wash the boys off of you."

"Yes, most definitely. I'm still feeling a touch intoxicated from last night, thus presumably smell of alcohol."

"Yes, you do," Kendra said smiling. "Ozzy, it's wonderful to see you genuinely happy."

"I appreciate that. For the first time in my life I feel authentic."

"It shows."

"Kendra, I've figured out the first step in my Plan B. In all honesty, it's now my Plan A."

"Tell me."

"I'm not going back. After tasting this life, I could never go back to living that lie."

THURSDAY | 23 OCTOBER | 10:30 EST
Latitude = 24.5599, Longitude = -81.7776
Fifth Street Baptist Church, 1311 Fifth Street
Key West, Florida

"Good morning, Roger. Please, come in and have a seat."

The aging Pastor Walton welcomed Roger into his office, directing him to the straight-backed, Shaker-style wooden chair opposite his meticulously organized desk. Pastor Walton noticed the expression on Roger's face. It appeared to be one of bemusement.

"Thank you, Pastor, for meeting with me on such short notice."

"What is it that's bothering you, son?"

"When I called earlier this morning, I was seeking your guidance regarding my relationship with Lacey, the woman I've been dating."

"Yes. I recall you speaking of her."

Roger nervously glanced around the room as he adjusted himself in the parochially uncomfortable chair. His eyes darted upward to fixate on a poster of the Lord taped to the cement block wall behind Pastor Walton's desk. Circling Jesus's head like a crown of prickly truth were the words, *Let him who is without sin cast the first stone.* Reading that verse, Roger jerked, arching his back as if to sit at attention.

Observing Roger's intense reaction, Pastor Walton softly said, "Cuts straight to the heart, doesn't it?"

Every drop of blood rushed from Roger's face, leaving him pale and moist. "You really have no idea, Pastor."

"What do you mean, Roger?"

"Let me put it this way. Do you believe God speaks to us?"

"If I didn't, I wouldn't be in this business. I believe God reaches out to us in any number of ways. Even in the sound of the wind passing through the palm trees, God's voice is everywhere."

Suiting Roger's mood, the morning was gloomy and damp. After experiencing a long and sleepless night, he arrived early at the church for his appointment with Pastor Walton. Perspiring, frustration devoured him. Physically fatigued and emotionally drained, Roger sought refuge by stopping in the sanctuary to pray.

"Okay, God! You've got my attention."

Roger had long sought the comfort of a companion. The one aspect of his world he had long proven to be a consummate failure. "Are they all crazy? Every one of them? Seriously, God? What was so wrong with Lacey?"

Roger could only assume God was witholding the gift of companionship as punishment for his failings. Fighting back the tears that began to fill his eyes, Roger grappled with the truth he had long buried under the force of his all consuming pride.

"Is it me, Lord?"

Desperate for answers, Roger pulled a Bible from the pew. In hopes of a landing on a revelation, he randomly opened God's Word and began to read the first verse his eyes captured, a familiar verse, one he had known since childhood.

Let him who is without sin cast the first stone.

That verse struck him as if he was reading it for the first time. Awakened by newfound wisdom, looking upward to the heavens, Roger spoke. "That cuts straight to the heart."

Calm fell upon him. Clarity of thought opened his heart.

"It's me, isn't it Lord? I'm the one throwing stones."

"I believe God spoke to me while I was praying in the worship hall this morning. Is that crazy, Pastor?"

"It'd be crazy not to listen when you feel God is speaking to you."

"The message He gave me was, *Let him who is without sin cast the first stone.*"

"Seriously?"

"My response was, *Cuts straight to the heart,* like you just said."

"That's truly amazing. How beautiful it is when God makes Himself known to us. What do you believe He was saying to you, Roger?"

"I know my resentment stands in the way of me finding inner-peace."

"I would agree, Roger."

"Lately, my guilt about something has intensified, to the point I can't ignore it any longer." Roger shifted in his chair as he faced the truth. "I know what I've got to do, Pastor. But how do I forgive someone who has let me down in the worst possible way?"

"Your Uncle Nestor?"

"You knew?"

"I've known you and your family for decades. Of course I knew. You understand, you're asking me how to forgive someone for a mistake made years ago?"

"You make it sound like it was a little mistake."

"No. I'm reminding you that it was decades ago. All of us have lapses in judgment, Roger. That's human nature."

"But you have to admit, some bigger than others."

"All have sinned and fallen short. A sin is a sin, no matter the degree."

Confessing, Roger said, "I've been punishing him, haven't I?"

"I believe you know the answer to that."

"I don't know if I have the nerve to approach him after all these years."

"I'm certain you can, Roger. Meditate on the message God gave you, then go and speak with your Uncle Nestor. I trust the Lord will lead you both to a place of healing."

"I will, Pastor. Right now."

.43

"That's gotta be her!" Kendra said, rushing toward the bar, attracting the attention of the more lackadaisical local crew.

"Must be, with that head of beautiful red hair."

"Seriously, Oswald? You call that beautiful?"

"You must admit, she is an attractive woman."

"We'll see how she looks after I'm through with her."

"Perhaps I should be the one to do the talking," Oswald said.

Kendra's demeanor toughened as she observed Lacey cheerfully stroll around the bar in their direction.

"Welcome to Schooner Wharf. What can I get you two?" Lacey said, sizing up her new customers, an unlikely pair. The older gentleman could easily be the boss. The other, her competition.

"Just a Coke for me," Oswald said.

"Really, Oswald, no hair of the dog? Well, you can get me a Bloody."

"Alright, fine," he said, "a Bloody Mary for me, as well."

Taking her own sweet time in preparing their drinks, she also prepared for battle. Returning with cocktails in hand, Lacey glared directly at Kendra.

"Would you like me to start you a tab, or don't you intend to stay?"

"I'll pay now," Kendra said. "This shouldn't take long."

Oswald observed Kendra's claws coming out and stepped in to prevent casualties. "You don't know us, but—"

"I believe I do," Lacey said. "Since you're Oswald, that makes you Kendra."

"I take it Jake knows we're here," Kendra said.

"Jake? You mean Blake."

"Is that what he told you? I'm not surprised."

"What's that supposed to mean?"

"Oh, sweetie. If a man lies to you about his name, don't you know he's likely to lie about everything?"

"Listen here, Kendra. From what I've heard, you're the last one who should be offering advice when it comes to men."

"Well, you little—"

"Don't even go there," Lacey said, postured for the attack. "Tell you what, why don't you take your drinks and move on out of here before I have you helped off the property?"

"Okay ladies, we obviously share a common concern for Jake, or Blake, whatever. So, let's all calm down a little and discuss this like mature adults. Lacey, I don't know what he's told you, but Jake is in grave danger. It's imperative we speak with him."

"He has no interest in speaking with you. Particularly you, Kendra."

Quickly placing his hand on Kendra's shoulder to subdue, Oswald said, "At least get a message to him. We're staying at the

Cypress House. It's imperative he contact us there. And Lacey, you need to tell him it's a matter of life and death."

"I don't have a way of getting ahold of him," Lacey said. "He left for Miami as soon as he heard Kendra was on the island."

"I don't believe a word you say, you little redheaded slut."

"From what Blake tells me, you're the slut," Lacey said, raising her upper lip in contempt. "Not even a very good one, at that."

"Tell you what, bitch," Kendra said before being cut off by Oswald.

"Come on, Kendra. This isn't getting us anywhere. Grab your drink and let's get out of here."

"Fine with me. The stench of that ferret is nauseating." Kendra eyed Lacey as she reached for her cocktail. "All I've got to say is, go screw yourself, you bloody whore," she said, dousing Lacey with her Bloody Mary before turning to strut away.

.44

"At least you didn't kick her teeth in," Oswald said.

"Impressed, huh? I even refrained from calling her the C-word."

"Classy move, Kendra."

"Was she playing me? Jake wouldn't have made me out as a slut."

"She was playing you, alright."

"I should go back there right now and take that bitch out."

"Kendra, don't you think you've done enough damage for one day?"

"I wish I'd done more."

"Watching your Bloody Mary drip off her face was quite the crescendo."

"You think Jake really left town?"

"I wouldn't be surprised," Oswald said, "and not because of you."

"I disagree. That bitch wouldn't have told us where he was going."

"Damn, you're right."

"Should you have mentioned the," Kendra deepened her voice, "*this is a matter of life and death* thing?"

"That may be what forces his hand. He's familiar with the CoK Protocol."

"So, what's our next move?"

Oswald took a moment to think. "I believe I should stake out the Schooner Wharf in hope that Jake will make contact with Lacey. That means you'll want to stay at the inn in case he shows up."

"Why don't you hang around the inn and I'll—"

"Forget about it, Kendra. I don't need to be bailing your bum out of the brig on top of everything else."

.45

"Hey, Lacey. What's going on?"

"She's a real piece of work."

"They found you already? That didn't take long."

"Yep. Here and gone in ten minutes flat."

"Should I ask how it went?"

"I just finished rinsing the last of Kendra's Bloody Mary out of my hair, if that gives you a clue."

"No way. She tossed a drink on you?"

"Sure did."

"Lacey, I'm sorry I got you mixed up in this."

"You're lucky I even called you."

"Why?"

"Because you lied to me."

"Lied? About what?"

"Seriously, Blake. You really don't know?"

"No."

"Let me put it this way, Jake."

"Oh, shit. That. I seem to have forgotten to mention that little detail."

"Why'd you keep up an alias with me?"

"Names can be confusing and a little complicated."

"Everything about you is a little complicated."

"I only used it to avoid fallout from my past."

"Obviously that didn't work," Lacey said.

"True, but I wasn't intentionally trying to mislead you."

"Your boss suggested I tell you to get in touch with him, as a matter of life and death."

"Seriously?"

"I don't know. You tell me. Is your situation a matter of life and death?"

"I'm not sure. Did he mention anything about a CoK?"

"No. What's that?"

"It's complicated."

"Like your name."

"Worse. What else did he say?"

"That they're staying at the Cypress House."

"You told them I left town, right?"

"I did."

"Did they appear to believe you?"

"I was pretty convincing."

"Good. Hopefully they bought it."

"Doc, I've got to get back to work."

"Before you go, tell me, have you spoken with Gus?"

"He and Rita usually roll in around noon. Don't worry, I'll test the waters as soon as I see him."

"You've really come through for me, Lacey."

"To be honest, this is pretty exciting stuff given my routine life."

"As long as it stays exciting and not deadly," I said.

"I assume that's a joke."

"Let's hope. We're getting together tonight, right?"

"If you promise to explain what's really going on?"

"That's a deal. And don't forget to bring the offshore account information. Better I get on it right away. I'm not going to be able to stick around Key West much longer."

"I've already pulled out the documents," she said. "Give me a call later."

"Will do."

"Be careful, will you, Doc?"

"Promise. They're likely to be tracking your moves. I'd guess they're on foot, so best if you take a taxi home today."

.46

"I figured I would find you here."

Kelley was anchored, vodka tonic in hand, at the bar lined with a collection of pretty boys and old queens, along with a few unsuspecting tourists who surprisingly weren't clued in by the bar's pink exterior and the rather tall, well-dressed *ladies* standing out front.

"You're not in hiding?"

"No. They wouldn't make a scene in public. That's why we're called secret agents, silly." I tossed a bag down on the bar in front of Kelley. "Here, I got you a present."

Kelley peeked inside the bag. "A cell phone. For me?"

"It's somewhat a selfish gift. With the noose being tightened around my neck, I may need to get in contact with an ally should things get dicey."

"Dicey?"

"They interrogated Lacey at her job this morning. My boss, Oswald, informed her that my situation is a matter of life and death."

Shocked, Kelley blurted out, "You really think they'd kill you?"

With that, he'd drawn the attention of both the bartenders and a number of nearby afternoon drunks. I laughed and briskly slapped him on the back in an effort to play it off as a joke.

"Kelley, keep it down."

"Sorry." Now speaking in a whisper, he asked again. "Would they? Kill you?"

"In the Agency there's a protocol that's assigned to dangerous targets and, on rare occasions, rogue agents. It's called a CoK, meaning Capture or Kill. If they can't take me in, they'll take me out."

"Oh, my! Aren't you scared?"

"Being tracked for the kill is never a comfortable situation, but it's something I've experienced a time or two. I can handle it."

"How did they know about Lacey? Are her ex-boyfriend and the police involved?"

"I really doubt the cops are involved. CIA works alone. As for their knowing about Lacey, that was my screw up. I mentioned her in a voicemail I left a friend back in Wisconsin. When I was drunk, of course."

"Pretty stupid mistake for a smart guy."

"Thanks for pointing that out."

"What's your next move?"

"I'm working on an escape plan."

"You're leaving the island?"

"Got to. Not only the island, I'm looking for a way out of the country. Possibly to Cuba."

"Is there anything I can do to help?"

"I'd appreciate it if you'd grab my clothes and stuff for me. I prefer not to go back to La Casa Cayo, as a precaution. "

"You've got it. I'll gather everything up," Kelley said.

"Perfect. When the time comes, I'm going to need you to bring me the steel case from under the house, too."

"Whatever you need."

"Here are the keys to the lock and my room. You can move in if you like. It's paid up for a month."

"Thank you, Blake. Not just for the room, but for trusting me."

"Trust among friends is everything. Sadly, in my business there aren't that many true friends around."

"At least now you've got me and Lacey."

"I've got you, Kelley. I only trust Lacey to a degree and that margin keeps getting smaller."

"What happened this time?"

"It's not important."

"I get it. It's that woman, the CIA agent. Isn't it?"

"Kendra? What do you mean?"

"You like that she's come looking for you."

"Come looking to kill me."

"Now that she's here, you're thinking about her again, aren't you?"

"I don't know where you're getting this."

"You've already tracked her down, haven't you?"

"Who's the secret agent here, anyway?"

"So you have."

"Damn, Kelley, you are good. Yes, I've seen her. Oswald left word with Lacey where they're staying. I went over earlier and spotted her out by the pool."

"Did that little heart of yours go pitter-patter?"

"She looked good, that's for sure. But the crazy ones—"

"You still care."

"Stop it, Kelley. You don't know everything about me."

"Then why'd you go looking for her?"

"I don't know. I needed to see how it felt when I saw her again."

"And? Would you take her back?"

"If things were different, maybe, but that doesn't matter anymore. She's the enemy, now."

.47

"Why are we stopping here?"

Roger pulled into a parking space at the beach, facing out to sea. He had not spoken a single word since leaving police headquarters. Not atypical for him. He had his quiet moods. Yet this time, Rosalyn felt something was different. Roger's peaceful gaze expressed what his words had not.

"I've got news to share."

"I could tell you had something on your mind. Did you speak with Lacey?"

"That's not it, but I did speak with someone."

"Tell me, Roger. It's good news, right?"

"The best, Roz. The absolute best. You're not going to believe it, but I spent the afternoon with Uncle Nestor."

"Oh, my God! That's wonderful. I am so proud of you."

"Roz, it was like old times. He's that same man I loved and respected as a boy."

"I have prayed about this day for so long."

"I knew you would be happy for me, Roz."

"What happened? Why today?"

"I met with Pastor this morning. I'd intended to ask his advice on dealing with my anger towards Lacey. Once I got there, a voice inside of me said, *It's not Lacey you're angry with. You're angry with yourself.*"

"The Lord does speak to us," Rosalyn said.

"I know. And the counsel I got from Pastor Walton was right on point. I realized my lack of forgiveness was eating me up inside. By the end of our talk I knew what I had to do. So, I got in my car and went straight over to the cafe where Uncle Nestor hangs out."

"I bet he was beyond shocked."

"When I walked over to him, reaching out to shake his hand, he wrapped both arms around me. His first words, *I've missed you.* — I expected him to be angry with me, Roz."

Roger turned away to hide the tears streaming down his face. Rosalyn could not hold hers back, either. She took his hand.

"I got my uncle back. You know he's always been like a father to me."

"I know, baby. And your Uncle Nestor got his favorite nephew back."

"He invited me over for dinner next week. The invitation was also extended to you."

"You talked about me?"

"He brought your name up. I guess he's been following our careers from the newspaper reports and was impressed by what he's read about you."

"Tell him I'd be honored. If that's okay with you."

"You kidding? Having you there with me will make all the difference in the world."

THURSDAY | 23 OCTOBER | 18:09 EST
Latitude = 24.5547, Longitude = -81.8014
Lobo's Mixed Grill, Key Lime Square
Old Town, Key West

Waiting for my dinner order to be prepared, I reached for the buzzing cell phone that was stuffed in my back pocket. I ended up at Lobo's Mixed Grill on the advice of a street vendor selling her handmade jewelry along Duval Street. A hidden gem, chill and friendly, this open air restaurant was tucked away right off Old Town's main drag, yet seemed miles away from its madness.

"Hello."

"Hey, Doc. It's Lacey. What are you up to?"

"Stopped to grab a bite to eat. I'm glad you called. I was just sitting here wondering if you've had a chance to speak with Gus?"

"Sure did. That's why I'm calling. He said you're more than welcome to join them."

"Cuba still part of their itinerary?"

"I believe that's the plan."

"Excellent."

"Why Cuba?"

"I have a contact there that can be trusted. Plus, given our government's current position on Cuba, I won't be running into too many Americans."

"I'm jealous. I've always wanted to go to Cuba before they make it legal," she said. "Anyway, Gus suggested we all meet up tonight to talk about it."

"Works for me."

"He'll pick us up by dinghy at the seaport to head out to the Gypsy Rose."

"What time?"

"He prefers to get out of the harbor before sunset."

"Does that mean we'll be spending the night?"

"Definitely. You wouldn't want to come back to town in a dinghy with Captain Gus after he's tied one on, which he does just about every night."

"Good to know. What do you think? Seven-thirty?"

"Sure, I'll let him know. Why don't you come over to my place first and we can walk there together."

"Sounds good. What should I bring our hosts?"

"Captain Morgan is a safe bet with those two."

"Want me to pick up anything for you?"

"I'm thinking it's a vodka night."

"You got it," I said thinking, for Lacey, it's always a vodka night. "Hey, my food's here already."

"Then go eat."

"Alright, I'll see you in a bit."

"Okay. See you shortly, baby."

Baby? My pet name has advanced from Doc to baby? I heard it in her voice. Lacey's pursuit of my affection had escalated. Proof that risk has a way of intensifying the passion of one's romantic affairs.

.49

Kendra freshened up for the evening after a long afternoon lounging poolside. Discouraged that Jake had not made contact, she drenched her emotions with a few too many cocktails at happy hour. Copping a not-so-happy buzz, she had an attitude.

"It's about time you came back," Kendra said as Oswald joined her by the pool. "Where've you been all day? Out chasing boy tail?"

"No. I told you I was going to tail Lacey."

"Well?"

"She left by taxi. I couldn't keep up on foot."

"How long ago was that?"

"She left a little after four."

"So what have you been doing since?"

"Looking for Jake. Why the interrogation, may I ask? Are you drunk?"

"I've had a couple," she said.

"I'd say a couple. So, no word from Jake?"

"Duh. You know I would've called you. Damn, Oswald, I think I liked you better in the closet. You're so flighty now."

"Kendra, you getting all pissy isn't going to help matters."

"Having me sit around this pool all day isn't either. We need a better plan of action. We're running out of time."

"What do you suggest we do?"

"You should've let me press the issue with Lacey."

"In your state of mind? I don't think so."

"This island's not that big. If I start asking questions around town, showing Jake's photo to some bartenders, I bet I could get a better lead on him. I'll play it as the jealous girlfriend looking for her man."

"Since he already knows we're here, it's worth a try."

"I'm going off on my own then. I don't need my dad following me around bar to bar."

"Agreed," Oswald said.

"What are you going to do tonight? Hang out at the gay bars? You sure as hell won't find him there."

"I believe I'll start with Stephen, the night manager. He found out where Lacey works rather quickly. Perhaps a little bribe will motivate him to get us additional information."

"I wouldn't do that, but whatever you think," Kendra said.

"Why not?"

"It's a small town. Locals aren't about to tell you too much about one of their own. Especially with a bribe. He'll think you're up to no good."

"We are up to no good, missy. And I believe money will speak very clearly to Stephen. This is the kind of town where people survive on tips."

"Have it your way."

"I can handle my own investigative strategies," he said.

"While you were out accomplishing absolutely nothing, I did my research on Key West's nightlife. I compiled a list of the kind of joints where Jake would hang. Locals' spots, wine bars, places known for their music scene."

"So, you're telling me you're going out partying?"

"Whatever you want to call it, Ozzy."

"Well, have fun, and should you happen to cross paths with the little redhead, do try to hold your temper."

.50

THURSDAY | 23 OCTOBER | 20:10 EST
Latitude = 24.5718, Longitude = −81.8089
Aboard the Gypsy Rose, The Gulf of Mexico
Off the Coast of Key West, Florida

"Thanks for having me aboard, Captain. You too, Rita."

Gus quietly cleared his throat, which led to a full-on cigarette-induced cough attack. Taking a swig of his drink to help soothe his throat, he said, "Lacey tells me you know your way around a sailboat."

"I've got a little experience under my belt."

"It'll sure be handy to have an extra mate on board."

"I'll just be glad to have someone other than the old fart to talk to," Rita said.

I glanced around the vessel, my escape craft, with intent. The Gypsy Rose had definitely seen better days. Not that she appeared to be unsafe, just tired and worn, much like her captain. The deck's varnish was peeling from the intense heat and constant spray of saltwater, her sails shared a history of harsh winds tugging at her seams, and her hull exposed the distinct markings of on-going repair. Even her insignia, a hand-painted yellow rose, had nearly faded into oblivion.

"She may not look like much," Gus said, noticing my scrutiny, "but she'll get us there."

"That's all that matters," I said. "Cuba won't be taking you out of your way, will it?"

"Not at all. It's on our itinerary, but with you on board, our route won't take us straight into Cuba. Lacey mentioned you've got a little problem. An issue between you and the United States government, I understand."

Gus paused. I kept my mouth shut. This was the point in our conversation I would learn his true feelings about aiding and abetting a wanted man.

"The way I see it," he said, "that only makes for a more interesting journey."

"I'm happy to hear you feel that way."

"Now, mind you, we'll need to take precautions. I'll explain, but I need my charts. Let's go down below," he said. "Ladies, if you'll excuse us."

I followed Gus down the ladder to the well stocked and perfectly organized galley. Gus proceeded to elaborate on the wonders of Cuba and its people as he poured us both a glass of Cuban rum. Pulling a number of nautical charts from their stowage, he continued with an elaborate synopsis of the political climate between the United States and Cuba, emphasizing his hopes that one day it would be a free and open nation. Even if that would, in his opinion, ultimately ruin the essence of Cuban culture.

After offering a toast, Gus said, "First of all, you realize this isn't a free ride."

"I would never expect that. I'm prepared to pay you a fair price for your services."

"I'm not talkin' money. Covering your share of expenses is all I ask. I'm talking about work. Sailing isn't all fun and games. It's a serious way of life."

"Certainly, Captain, I'll carry my weight. I'm just thankful you agreed to take me along."

"Rita and I love having company. We've been trying for years to get Lacey to come, but that girl sure can get stuck in her ways. I don't think she's left the island since she got here."

He unrolled a map of the Florida Straights and Caribbean Sea. "Here we are," he pointed to Key West. "Since I'll have a fugitive on board, we'll need a neutral location as our first port of call. The Bahamas, being the closest, is the logical choice."

"Neutral location?"

"With you along, it'd be far too risky to sail straight into Cuba, and not nearly as much fun. We'll need to have papers filed to show we'll be sailing to a legal destination. That way, it's less likely the Coast Guard will board us for inspection." Next, he unrolled a map of Cuba across the galley table. "Having you on board will also dictate our port of entry into Cuba. I suggest Playa Santa Lucía, on the northern coast. It's popular with the European travelers." Gus slid the map around to more closely examine that region. "Here. This is where we'll make land," he said pointing to Playa Santa Lucía. "Being a resort area, we'll blend right in."

"You speak as if you've done this before, carried illegal cargo, that is."

"Usually only Cuban rum and cigars. There have been rare occasions when a friend needed a hand escaping their past."

"I can't wait to hear those stories."

"Once we're underway, you and I'll have plenty of time to burn telling our tales."

Returning to the deck following our planning session, and of course, more Cuban rum, we gathered at the aft to relax and enjoy the darkening sky. Gus reclined in his hammock strung between the masts, and Rita sat legs-crossed on the deck next to him. We munched on coconut meat, fresh pineapple and cheese while our hosts shared stories of their nautical adventures.

As the hours passed, Lacey's affections for me flowed more freely. Now snuggled comfortably next to me, I couldn't determine if her attraction was honorable or merely hormonal. She ran her hand up and down my back while occasionally lifting her head upward to gently kiss my neck.

"I don't know about the rest of you," Rita said, "but I'm going to need to hit the rack and call it a night."

"Me, too. These old bones need their rest," Gus said, pulling himself from his hammock, struggling to maintain his balance as he slid down to the deck. "Your quarters are in the bow. Feel free to stay up as long as you like. You won't be bothering us. Rita will pass out in minutes and once I take my hearing aid out I can't hear a thing."

"Since I'm the only one who has a job, I better turn in, too.," Lacey said. "Gus, you'll be up in time to take me back to shore for my shift, won't you?"

"Don't you worry. I'm up with the sun. Good night, kids. Don't do anything I wouldn't do."

Lacey went off to our quarters ahead of me, wishing to have a few minutes alone to get ready for bed. I grabbed a bottle of water and peered out into the dark of night. My future was once again secured. My freedom remained. Everything I ever wanted was advancing with each new encounter. I was living the dream. Doing exactly as I chose, with ease, carving out my path to destiny.

Reflecting on the evening's events, I realized Lacey had become ever more suggestive as the night progressed. Taking another gulp of ice cold water, I began imagining her, down below, awaiting my arrival to bed. My body shivered with desire.

Being gently rocked by the ocean's subtle motion, my mind drifted to recall her words. *With you leaving so soon, our love affair is going to be short-lived. We've got to make every moment count. Starting tonight.*

On the verge of getting exactly what I had hoped for, I knew it was not consistent with the truth I'd come on this journey to find. I couldn't put our romance in high gear simply because the end of our fling had a deadline. I'd merely be using her as a substitution for love. And her, me. It would be living out a lie. A fun lie, but a lie, none the less.

Having out waited the sandman, Lacey was fast asleep. Her soft wimpers of a snore lofted upwards to Gus's hammock where I now lay. Closing my eyes, my thoughts turned to Jake's life and his lover.

FRIDAY | 24 OCTOBER | 07:58 EST
Latitude = 24.5594, Longitude = -81.8031
Outside Cypress House, Off Dey Street
Key West, Florida

I got off easy. Lacey didn't wake up when I turned in. Admittedly, she had more than her share of vodka. Yet, in the morning's harsh light, on our dinghy ride in, she whispered the same erotic offer posed during last night's merriment. In her excited state, at such an early hour, Lacey was already confirming her choice for the evening's entertainment—the Green Parrot Bar, ten o'clock. Back on land, my first order of business was a visit to the Cypress House.

Oswald, after completing a hefty, but not so healthy bacon, egg and pastry breakfast, exited the property precisely at eight forty-seven. Kendra's curtains had yet to be drawn to allow morning to enter the room. Catching her asleep was my hope.

Working my way over the block wall that enclosed the Cypress House compound, I skillfully avoided detection by the breakfast crowd. Wedged between the end of the building and the perimeter wall, I shimmied my way up to her balcony. Remaining prone until reaching her door, I quietly unlatched the lock with my knife and entered her room. There, she lay sleeping before me, causing my heart to skip a beat.

⊕

"I guess I have some explaining to do."

Kendra wiped her eyes, focusing on the shadowy figure standing at the edge of her bed.

"What the—"

"It's okay, baby. It's only me."

"Jake!" She jumped from the bed and rushed to my open arms. "I've missed you."

"I've missed you, too," I said, the words falling out of my mouth without due consideration.

"You're lucky I didn't shoot your ass sneaking in here on me like that!"

"I already grabbed your gun from under the mattress. I know your habits."

"You think you're smooth, don't you? I'm just not sure how long your luck is going to hold out."

"What's that supposed to mean?"

"They'll put a CoK on your head if you don't return before all hell breaks loose."

"A CoK? Me?" I said.

"Oswald told me that's the Protocol required should you ever go AWOL."

"I'm not surprised."

"Not surprised? What in the hell are you involved with? Not only that, why in the hell did you skip out on me, without a single word? And furthermore, what in the hell are you doing with that, that—Lacey? Really? Her?"

"Slow down, Kendra. Take a breath."

"What were you thinking? That you could just walk away from your responsibilities? Everything was fine."

"Everything was not fine," I said. "It wasn't real. We were mere game pieces waiting on their next move."

"Damn you, we weren't a game!"

"Maybe not, Kendra, but everything else in our world sure as hell was."

"What are you saying? Were we or weren't we?"

"It doesn't matter, Kendra. I had no other choice. I had to leave for my own sanity."

"It does matter. Were we a game?"

I gave in. "No, baby, we weren't. You know that."

"Oh, Jacob."

Kendra took my hand, pulling me along as she returned to the bed. She struggled to remove my t-shirt.

"Kendra—"

"Not a word."

"But we—"

"I told you. Not a word."

I surrendered, under threat of pleasure. We embraced. Her kiss, like coming home.

"Is this where you make a point of reminding me it was only sex?" Kendra hid her face beneath the top sheet, for protection of sorts.

"Only sex? Only the most amazing sex."

"Dammit, Jake. Will you give me a straight answer for once?"

It wasn't breakup sex, nor was it casual. It was, however, an awakening of emotion. The thoughts that followed caused my conflicting worlds to collide. Lying safely next to her, I battled. It wasn't the comfort of the familiar, it wasn't the joy we shared, it wasn't even the love we had sustained through adversity. It wasn't any one thing that made me want her. It was simply everything. The problem, going back to my old life was not an option, which meant Kendra could not be an option.

"I can't keep doing it, Kendra."

"Being with me?"

"Not you. The lie. I can't go on serving as the Agency's pawn."

"Jake, you know they'll never stop looking for you."

"Trust me. I've got a damn good plan in the works. Where I'm going, they'll never find me."

"You're not going to tell me where, are you?"

"That wouldn't be wise."

"Now I'm the enemy," she said.

"Sleeping with the enemy. Just like old times, huh?" I said.

The jagged slice of those cutting words, my subconscious offensive intended to deflect love's pursuit, left Kendra wounded. She jerked, abruptly pulling away, taking the covers along with her.

"Jake, you suck! You know I'm not proud of my past, and you had to rub my nose in it. Again!"

There is a rather apropos verse engraved in the foyer of CIA Headquarters: *You shall know the truth, and the truth will make you free.* A reminder of the reason for my escape. Though my journey was one of seeking freedom, truth was required. Being truthful with Kendra would mean being so with myself. And the truth is, I wasn't withdrawing because of her past, I was running from my own, leaving Kendra a casualty of the warring factions within my soul.

"You're right, Kendra. I do suck. I'd tell you I didn't mean it, but I've come to realize I once did." Kendra's body now turned away, I moved closer to spoon her, gently stroking her hair.

"Not anymore?"

"Not anymore," I said. "At one time, I was troubled by your past, for doing the exact same things I'd done myself."

"I wish I could learn to let go of my past."

"I know you can, baby. The past belongs in the past. Keep it there. Guilt only steals—"

A knock at the door stopped me in mid-thought.

"Who is it?" Kendra said.

"Oswald. Do you have company?"

"The TV. I turned it down. What do you need?"

"I have a fresh lead on Jake I want to tell you about. I can't wait to get my hands on him."

"I'm getting ready to jump in the shower. I'll stop over as soon as I'm finished."

"I'll be down by the pool, See you there, and don't dilly dally."

Giving Oswald plenty of time to move on, I said, "That was awkward. He can't wait to get his hands on me? Oswald wouldn't take me out, would he?"

"Not without first explaining, in great detail, why he had to."

"That's comforting. For now, it's best we keep this visit between us."

"You know I will," she said.

"Oh, yeah. About Oswald. He's gay?"

"Can you believe it? How'd you know?"

"I was less than five feet away from him at a gay bar."

"Just what were you doing at a gay bar?"

"Long story. How'd you figure it out?"

"After the fiasco with us, he came out to me. I believe he's pretty much ready to drop out of circulation, too.

"About the fiasco with us. I left you hanging. Pretty shitty, huh? Guess I just wasn't thinking."

"You didn't want to think about anyone but yourself."

"I'm trying to break that habit. Part of the new me," I said.

"I already see a difference in you. You seem more, I don't know, content."

"You seem pretty content, yourself," I said.

"I am now. I'm laying next to the only man I've ever loved for the right reason."

I pulled her close.

"Come on lover boy. Let's go take a shower."

52

FRIDAY | 24 OCTOBER | 10:29 EST
Latitude = 24.5610, Longitude = -81.8019
Schooner Wharf Bar, The Historic Seaport
Key West, Florida

"Roger. What a surprise."

Roger casually strolled up to the Schooner Wharf's bar to where Lacey stood warily waiting. Her boisterous greeting, amplified by nervousness, alerted the entire bar staff of his arrival.

"How have you been, Lacey?"

"I'm doin'." Looking up at Roger, truly paying attention, she noticed the calm expression on his face. "Wow, you look good."

"I feel good," he said.

"So, what's up?"

"I came by to apologize. I had some personal issues boiling up inside of me and took it out on you in the process."

"Yeah, I believe you did."

"Sorry for being such a jerk."

"Apology accepted."

"You know, if you think about it, we weren't a good match for one another," Roger said.

"We're different fish, that's for sure. That doesn't mean we can't be friends."

"I'd like that. I enjoy your carefree nature, especially now that you're not my responsibility."

Lacey let it go.

"Tell me, Roger. What's got you feeling so good?"

"I spoke with my Uncle Nestor."

"You did? That's wonderful news. How'd it go?"

"You can't imagine. It was just like it used to be."

"Good for you, and your uncle. You got plans to get together again?"

"Sure do. He invited me over for dinner. Well, me and Rosalyn."

"Rosalyn, really?"

"Guess I better apologize for sending her in my place. You know that's not like me. I was being a little crazy at the time."

"All is forgiven and forgotten."

"Rosalyn's the one who talked sense into me about how I was treating you."

"Us girls know."

"Sometimes us guys know, too. Like with your friend. I'm convinced his story is much more than he lets on."

"Roger, come on. I honestly don't believe he's a criminal."

"Let's hope I'm off base."

"There's a first time for everything."

An awkward pause lingered.

"Um," Roger stammered, "could I stop over sometime to get my gun? I mean, if you don't feel you need it."

"No, I don't need a gun. I'll grab it for you right after work. I forgot and left it aboard the Lucky Dog the other night. It fell out of my backpack while we were sailing. Doc probably thought I was the criminal at that point. He shut it in the cabinet by the helm for safe keeping."

"Then don't bother. I'll get over there and pick it up."

Roger lifted his hand up to his ear indicating to Lacey he was receiving a radio call. He listened intently. "I need to go. Duty calls."

"I'm glad you stopped by. I sure feel a whole lot better now that we've talked."

"Me too, friend." Wanting to gloat, Roger found a way to mention his new acquisition. "Let me know if you want to take my boat out again, that is, while I still have her. She's up for sale."

"Really? You're selling the Lucky Dog?"

"Uncle Nestor has a beautiful old schooner he doesn't much use these days. He thinks she needs a captain that can properly care for her."

"Sweet. Congratulations."

"Gotta run. You take good care, Lacey."

"You, too. I'll see you around town."

53

FRIDAY | 24 OCTOBER | 11:08 EST
Latitude = 24.5593, Longitude = -81.8032
Cypress House, 601 Caroline Street
Key West, Florida

"See, that didn't take long," Kendra said as she descended to the chaise lounge situated next to Oswald.

"You must have slept like a princess last night. You are absolutely glowing, girlfriend."

"I'm feeling pretty damn good. I don't know why, but from the moment I woke up this morning I've felt orgasmic."

"Oh? Did you meet a replacement for Jake last night?"

"What would make you say something so mean? No, I did not!"

"Sorry. Must be the island breeze or something," he said.

"You mentioned a lead?"

"Yes, the lead. I've obtained information that could help direct us to where Jake is staying."

"How?"

"This being such a small town certainly helped. I stopped to tour the Hemingway House during my morning walk. Beautiful gardens, and lots of six-toed cats. And you know how I feel about cats. Anyway, I struck up a conversation with one of the tour guides, mentioning I'd hoped to locate an old friend that recently moved here. I showed him a picture of Jake on my phone and the gentleman was certain he'd seen him the past several days walking up Whitehead Street from the direction of the Southernmost Point. Always in the early afternoon."

"Good lead," Kendra said. "If it's okay with you, I'll scope out that neighborhood and you can keep working the interviews."

"That's what I'd prefer. I'm finding it rather enjoyable chatting with the locals. They all seem to have an odd, almost numb sense of contentment. I can see it in their eyes."

"Maybe they're just stoned."

54

FRIDAY | 24 OCTOBER | 13:15 EST
Latitude: 24.5583, Longitude: –81.7874
KWPD Headquarters, North Roosevelt Boulevard
Key West, Florida

Roger stood in the doorway of the station's crime lab with an evidence bag tightly gripped in his hand. The young and ambitious lab technician, Alex Greene, jumped to his feet to properly address his superior.

"Detective Morales, what can I do for you?"

"I have a favor to ask. A confidential favor."

"Absolutely, sir. Whatever I can do."

Roger displayed his .45 caliber Ruger through the protective plastic bag. "This is my firearm. I'd like you to run the prints."

"Your pistol, sir? Was it stolen?"

"No, nothing like that. A person of interest handled it recently and I'd like to know if he has a record."

"You realize the department hasn't been granted access to the FBI's Integrated Automated Fingerprint Identification System, yet. That'll greatly limit our chances for a hit. Unless," Alex strategically upped his value, "I call in a favor from a friend I've known since college. He's now with the Miami office of the Bureau."

"Whatever you need to do, but remember, not a word to anyone around here. Not even Detective Chapman. Got it?"

"Yes, sir."

"How long is this going to take?"

"Possibly sooner, but can I have until Monday? I know he's been busy as hell, lately."

"Monday's fine. If it's sooner, call me the minute you receive any information, day or night."

"Will do, sir."

"Alex, thank you. I do appreciate this, and I won't forget it, either."

FRIDAY | 24 OCTOBER | 22:51 EST
Latitude = 24.5541, Longitude = −81.8030
The Green Parrot Bar, Corner of Southard & Whitehead
Key West, Florida

Ranked as one of the Best Bars in America by the likes of *Playboy Magazine*, the Green Parrot is far from what one might expect from an establishment with such critical acclaim. By walking in the door of this legendary locals' favorite, it quickly becomes apparent that what you see is about all you're going to get. No trendy decor with comfortable, overstuffed chairs, no flashy cocktail waitresses wearing fishnets and high heels, nor a single dignified restroom valet to offer a fresh towel. What's earned this open-air drinkery on lists of distinction is its great music, good times atmosphere, and by holding true to one basic tenet: Never, ever, change too much, too fast.

The band had already taken the stage when I arrived to face a sea of patrons overflowing onto the sidewalk. I worked my way inside. Scanning the room, I sought out Lacey.

"Hey! There you are." I reached out to offer her the standard hug greeting. "Damn, the town is packed tonight."

"It's the weekend."

"That's right. The days seem to run together down here."

"As long as I can remember at least one thing I'm supposed to do each day, I figure I've still got a grasp on reality," she said.

"Guess you gotta keep the expectations as low as possible."

"Before I get buzzed up and forget, here's that offshore account information. I meant to give it to you last night on the Gypsy Rose, that is before I passed out on you. Don't you worry, I'll make that up to you tonight," Lacey said, while giving my derrière a tight squeeze.

Her intentions were obvious, her words distasteful. The sweet and familiar taste of Kendra's lips still consumed my every thought. At the moment, I didn't want some thieving, party girl hanging around. What I needed was my space.

"Excuse me for a few. I need to hit the men's room."

"Okay. Let's meet back up out on the porch. I need to take a break from the music. "

"Here baby, I got you a Corona," Lacey said as she walked up from behind me.

"Too funny. Here, I got you one, too."

"Guess we better drink up. — Cheers."

"Cheers."

After a hefty swig, Lacey said, "You'll never guess who stopped in work today."

"One of Key West's Finest?"

"You guessed it. I have to give him credit, he was very kind, and the most chill I've ever seen him."

"That's good."

"Yeah, but he still thinks you're trouble."

"Oh, I am."

"He apologized and said he's cool with being friends."

"Perfect. You're the last person who needs to be on the bad side of a cop."

"No shit."

"And it's over without a lot of drama," I said.

"It's over, alright. He even asked for his gun back."

"He did?"

"I told him I left it aboard the Lucky Dog and said where you stuck it."

"You specifically said that I put the gun away?"

"Yes. Why?"

"We've got a problem, Lacey."

"What?"

"As much as Roger wants to pin something on me, I know he'll have the prints run."

"You said you don't have a record."

"I don't, but under the new Homeland Security policies of collaboration, should my prints be run through the FBI's database, the system will automatically alert my past employer."

"Why is that a problem? They already know you're here."

"Oswald and Kendra know, but I'm sure they haven't notified our superiors. Not yet, anyway. But it's a problem for you, too."

"You think he'd run my prints, too?"

"They'll run them all."

"Holy shit!"

"We've got to get to the Lucky Dog, and now. There's always a chance he didn't grab it, yet."

"What if he has?"

"If he has, the rules of the game are going to change."

"Change how?"

"For one, we'll need to make you disappear. Tonight."

"Tonight?"

"You have no choice."

"Why tonight? I need time to think this through."

"Time is something you won't have. If Roger gets a hit on your prints, Love Lane will become a crime scene."

"What if he doesn't check that database? Won't it look suspicious if I skip out on work and disappear?"

"Smythers owes you one. Ask her to cover your shifts for a few days. Tell her you've got to go to Miami to help out a friend in crisis. That'll buy us the time we need to see what transpires."

"Slow down. I'm freaking out."

"I'll help you through this, but you've got to trust me and do as I say."

"I promise."

"Let's get out of here. For both our sakes, pray the gun is still there."

"I'm scared. I can't go to jail."

"I won't let that happen, but I need you to think. Where can you lay low for a few days without anyone knowing?"

"Let me think," she said, perspiration beading on her forehead. "I know. The Roman's place over on Angela Street. They're snowbirds from New York that I've known for years. They gave me a key to their place in case of an emergency. No one would have a clue we're there."

"That sounds perfect. Only I won't be staying. I need to move about freely, as long as possible. There's a lot to pull together should we need to make a fast escape. Conferring with Gus being my first order of business."

.56

"Scoot that cute little butt of yours over, will you? You're taking up the whole bed."

"You came back. I was just dreaming about you, Jacob."

I was drained from the evening's events. Roger had already gotten his gun, which was all Lacey needed to throw her into a complete meltdown. I couldn't blame her. She'd created a happy life on this island. The only consoling insight I had to offer was, *moving on is far better than giving up*. She added, *or living behind bars*. We were both right.

Lacey's selection of a safe house could not have been more ideal—overgrown tropical shrubs and trees obscured the front of the house, heavy plantation style shutters covered its windows and doors and, the icing on the cake, discreet access from an alleyway running behind the property.

We gathered the necessities for Lacey's life on the run, as well as enough food from her cabinets to survive on for a few days. As for Sinatra, his food was left on the neighbor's porch, along with a note that read,

> *Family emergency. Be back soon. Thanks for keeping*
> *watch of Sinatra.*
>
> *~ Lacey*

With Lacey feeling somewhat secure, I left her at the safe house, promising to return early the next day. I fled to the only place where my heart and my head could rest in agreement. In Kendra's presence, now fully entangled in her arms and legs, fully surrendered, I was at peace.

My defenses weakened from the intimacy we just shared, I risked seeking answers. "Do you really?"

"What?"

"Love me," I said.

"Don't you know, silly?"

"Why then do you push me away the moment I show any sign of attachment? The second I let down my guard and share my feelings—boom, you're as cold as ice."

"I know," she said. "I guess it's how I protect my heart."

"Well, it works."

"Jacob, give me another chance, I'll make it different this time. You're all I want. You're all I have."

"What can I do, Kendra? Look at my options. One, I give up and go back to a life I loathe, but I get the girl. That is if she doesn't push me away, again. The other, I live my dream of finally being free, but forever pine for the soulmate I left behind."

"You could take me with you."

"What, and make a federal felon out of you in the process? No way. I'm not dragging you down into the muck with me. You'd only end up a casualty of my need to run."

"I already am."

"I know you are, and it's not fair."

"Jake, listen. You don't want to be constantly looking over your shoulder. Come back with us and no one at the Agency would be any the wiser."

"That might not be the case," I said.

"What did you do now?"

"There's a good chance my fingerprints have been run by a Key West cop. Lacey's ex-boyfriend."

"Nice work. Now I see why they've always assigned your ass a fulltime handler. What were you thinking?"

"Well, I—"

"You weren't. How'd the cops get your prints?"

"Off a pistol he gave Lacey."

"This keeps getting better."

"You think that's funny? The ex-boyfriend has it out for me. He's convinced I'm a criminal. He'll definitely run the prints."

"Obviously, they won't find anything, but that won't prevent a flag being raised in the Agency," she said.

"That's not completely accurate. Chances are they'll get a hit on a wanted criminal."

"You're kidding me. What'd Lacey do?"

"Embezzlement. Apparently, she recovered funds her late husband's business partner had stolen from their firm."

"Is that all?"

"As far as I know."

"Jake, do you realize the interagency stir this is going to create? FBI will bust the Agency's balls over this for years."

"You think?"

"I've got to read Oswald in on this immediately. He deserves a heads up."

"Oswald plays by the rules. You know that. Give me one more day before you give me up."

"Jake, I honestly don't believe Oswald could take you out."

"Maybe not, but he'd likely go for the capture and that's a risk I'm not willing to take. All I need is a little more time to pull things together and I'll be gone."

"Gone?" Kendra asked, her eyes filling with tears. "You heartless bastard. How can it be so damn easy for you to walk away?"

Kendra turned away, tugging at the bed sheet to isolate herself in a cotton cocoon.

I awoke to a single ray of sunlight cutting through the split between the curtains. I wanted to defend myself. I wanted her to know I truly cared. I wanted to be able to tell her that I can finally admit it to myself, I'm in love with her. But, in my well-rehearsed style, I ran, leaving her asleep, alone, without answers.

.57

"Detective Morales. I apologize for hesitating to give you the results over the phone. Due to the delicate nature of the FBI's findings, I thought it best we discuss this face to face."

Alex had long wished to earn Roger's respect, a man whose favor carried weight in the department. A quick response to his superior's request could only bolster his status in the Detective's mind. However, the results of his rapid turnaround did not grant the glory Alex anticipated.

"Well, I'm here now. What's he wanted for?"

"That's the delicate part, sir. He's not wanted. He comes up clean. No record exists.

"Then do you want to tell me why I'm here?"

Alex walked across the room, shutting the door of the lab. He walked back to his desk and nervously picked up the file containing Lacey's FBI criminal identification report. "It's your girlfriend, sir. She's our match."

Roger stood stunned, drawing a mental picture of the ridicule he would soon be facing from his colleagues.

"For your information, she is no longer my girlfriend," Roger said. "Still, I have to admit, I am in shock. What'd they find?"

"For starters, her name isn't Lacey. It's Amber Uhrig of Hoboken, New Jersey. That's across the river from New York City."

"I know where Hoboken is. Just tell me what she's wanted for."

"It's a lengthy report that you'll probably want to read on your own, but the summary is, she's wanted on everything from conspiracy, fraud, money laundering, to murder."

"Murder! Lacey? Let me see that report."

Roger grabbed the file from Alex's hand. Flipping through the pages that detailed Lacey's criminal past, the veins in his temples bulged. Shaking his head, he folded the document and stuffed it in his back pocket.

"Alex, I'm going to need to go over this with Detective Chapman before proceeding. I trust you've told no one about it."

"Absolutely not, sir."

"Keep it that way. The other guys are going to have a heyday with this once it gets out."

"Yes, sir. They certainly are," Alex said.

"I wasn't asking for your input."

"Sorry, sir. Here's my friend's phone number. He said you'll need to coordinate your efforts with the Bureau."

"I'll put a call in to him later this afternoon. And Alex, even though it's not what I had anticipated, I still owe you one."

.58

"Kendra, do you want to tell me what's going on around here?"

"I have no idea what you're talking about."

"You most certainly do. At first I thought, perhaps you were talking to yourself. Then when the blatant sounds of sex were coming from your room the other morning, I attributed it to your going out and whoring around. But this morning's acrobatic performance, at five o'clock in the morning, mind you, most definitely included Jake's involvement. I know you too well. You wouldn't give up your precious sleep for anyone but Jake. That, and Jake's the only person you care enough about to bitch out following what sounded like amazing sex."

"You could hear all that?"

"This place was built in the 1800s. The walls aren't thick enough to contain that level of romp and ruckus," he said.

"I was going to tell you today. Jake asked me if I'd hold off until he—"

"Escapes, again? I don't like it any better than you, but we have a job to do."

"What? Kill Jake?"

"Convince him to return," he said.

"What do you think I've been doing?"

"Have you gotten anywhere?"

"Not really."

"He's not leaving us with many options."

"Worse," Kendra said, "you need to be prepared for a call from Langley."

"Langley?" Oswald said in a tone that drew the attention of the others who were enjoying their breakfast.

"Jake's fingerprints may have been run through the FBI's database by a Key West cop. That would send an alert to the Agency.

"I'm well aware of what it will do. How in God's name did the police get his prints?"

"It had something to do with that woman—Lacey."

"Why am I not surprised," he said.

"Before Jake, Lacey was dating a local cop who gave her the gun. Jake handled it and the cop found out."

"I swear, he has a knack for luring in the psycho ones that can only cause him headaches."

Ignoring Oswald's words, she said, "There's more to the mix. Lacey's wanted on embezzlement charges. So there's a real good chance, if the prints are run, she's busted."

"At the first sign the police are making a move on either of them, I will have no choice but to contact Langley."

"I understand."

"Should it come to that, I'll inform them we're already in pursuit of the rogue agent, Jake Lander, and that we have the situation under control. That should discourage them from sending additional assets down here to handle our problem for us."

"I'll arrange a meeting with Jake. Maybe you can get somewhere with him."

"No maybe. He'll listen, and he will return with us. Period."

"What if he refuses?"

"He has no other choice in the matter," Oswald said. "The alternative is a death sentence."

"No! You wouldn't, would you?"

"Under the circumstances, it's not so much a matter of who kills Jake, but a question of when he's killed. I'm in agreement it is far better if someone else pulls the trigger."

"Does that mean you'd be on board with helping him escape?"

"Escape? Are you serious? After this mess, my days with the Agency are surely numbered. I would appreciate the opportunity to enjoy my retirement somewhere other than from behind bars. Something you should consider, as well."

.59

"Rita, look who just showed up. Maybe now we'll get some straight answers."

Walking into the Schooner Wharf Bar was like walking into a wake. Solemn and quiet, the staff and regulars appeared perplexed and distressed.

"Damn, Gus. Who died?"

"Blake, glad you're here. You have any idea what's going on with Lacey?"

"What do you mean?"

"Detective Morales and his partner were just here asking all sorts of questions about her whereabouts. They even took a download of the bar's surveillance videos."

"Damn it! He ran the prints."

"Prints of what?" Rita said.

"Let's head out back. I'll explain."

Taking their cocktails with them, Rita and Gus followed me to the waterfront side of the bar. Reaching the edge of the rope-lined boardwalk overlooking the Gulf of Mexico, the three of us huddled, looking out to sea. I lowered my voice to an airy whisper.

"Fingerprints. The Detective lifted our prints from a gun Lacey was carrying when she and I went sailing."

"A gun," Rita said. "On your first date?"

"I know. Morales found out I handled it, and you know he wouldn't miss an opportunity to check out my background."

Looking puzzled, Gus said. "Then why were they more interested in Lacey than you?"

"I'm not in the FBI's database. Lacey is."

Rita's eyes wide open showed her shock. "The FBI?"

"That's why I'm here. She needs our help. Lacey's got to disappear, and soon."

"Whatever she needs, we're here for her," Rita said. "Isn't that right, Gus?"

"I told you, Rita. I figured all along that girl was running from the law. Do you know what she did?"

"Embezzlement."

"Embezzlement? That girl sure doesn't live like she's got money," Rita said.

"She hasn't been able to transfer any of the funds from an offshore account in the Cayman Islands," I said. "Gus, how soon can you be ready to leave port?"

"I'm still waiting on my new solar panels for the Gypsy Rose. I've been tracking the delivery status online. They should be here Monday morning. Once they're in my hands, we can set sail."

"That only gives us tomorrow to stock our provisions," I said, glancing toward Rita. "Is that enough time?"

"Don't you boys worry. I'll make sure we're ready for a Monday launch. High noon, as always."

"Thanks, Rita. Now, the logistics. We can't leave port together."

"You know Morales will have eyes on us," Gus said.

"We'll need to determine a rendezvous point a few miles out. A remote key, perhaps."

"Boca Grande Key, definitely," Gus said. "It's uninhabited and several miles out. That'd be the ideal place to pickup a couple of wayward passengers. But how are you and Lacey going to get there?"

"I'm still working out those details."

"I saw where Detective Morales put a 'For Sale' sign on the Lucky Dog," Rita said. "He might give you a good deal."

"Oh, I'm sure he would," I said. "Don't you worry, we'll find a way to Boca Grande."

"What time?" Gus asked.

"Give me a window of a few hours. Say, midnight to two, or maybe three, should we run into the unforeseen."

"Got it. Monday night, Tuesday morning," Gus said in clarification.

"Sounds like we've got a plan." Eager to get out of there to find a less obvious locale, I jotted down Kelley's phone number. "Expect a call from this number tomorrow to arrange for the drop of our luggage."

"How's Lacey coping?" Rita asked.

"She's coping. She knew this day might come. Lucky for her, and for me, we've got you two."

"We're happy to help you kids out," Gus said.

Rita smiled at me and said, "Lacey's sure lucky that you came along when you did. I don't believe she would've handled this very well on her own."

Gus butted in. "Rita, she wouldn't need this kind of help if he hadn't come along in the first place."

"'On that note, it's time for me to go," I said. "Thanks again for all you're doing for us."

"It's our pleasure, isn't it, Gus?"

"Yep, it's all good. We'll see you kids on Boca Grande."   " N o matter what you see out there, trust that we're going to show."

.60

"It's only me."

The safe house on Angela Street was musty and dark. A dim light drew me through the kitchen toward the living room where I found Lacey sitting on the sofa. Her eyes were swollen from tears, her face saturated with fear.

"There you are," Lacey said. "It seems like you've been gone for days. What's happening out there?"

"They know, Lacey."

"Are you positive?"

"Yes. Roger and his partner were at the Schooner Wharf today asking lots of questions."

"Jake, I'm frightened. You've got to get me out of here. I can't go to prison."

"I spoke with Captain Gus. He knows what's going on and is ready to help."

Placing her elbows on her knees and her head in her hands, Lacey stared down at the floor. Her voice was weak as she spoke. "There's more."

"More what?"

"More to the story of how I ended up here."

"I'm listening"

"You're going to hate me."

"I'm not going to hate you. Just tell me what you did."

"My husband's business partner, I told you he died in a car crash. That's not how it happened. I'm responsible for his death."

"Okay. Directly or indirectly responsible?"

"Directly. I shot him."

A bit stunned, I said, "For the money?"

"That, and paybacks. My husband, Nick, and his partner were doing business with a Colombian drug cartel. They ran the laundering operation that transferred drug money into legitimate investments. Only Nick's partner was moving some of their cash into an offshore numbered account. Nick figured it out right before the Colombians. When their thugs came for revenge, Nick's partner convinced them he was the one ripping them off. So, they murdered him."

"They didn't take out his partner, too? That's unusual."

"No. He assured them he could recover the money, if they gave him time. It was either the Colombians or me to get their hands on that cash. So I figured, why not me?"

"Why'd you kill him? The Colombians were bound to do the dirty work for you."

"That payback was all mine," Lacey's voice turned cold, and her eyes emotionless. "I wanted to watch him beg for his life. Even more, I wanted to see him suffer, the bastard."

Comprehending what Lacey just told me, I paced the floor. Until I had time to calculate how this new information would impact my escape, I had to play my cards with caution.

Lacey spoke up in her own defense. "That was over seven years ago. I'm a totally different person now."

"Do you still have the keys to Roger's boat?"

"They're in my backpack. Why?"

"I'm working on the specifics of our escape. I might need to borrow it for a night."

"How soon until I get out of here? Just sitting around this dark, depressing house is driving me insane."

"I'll come for you in a couple days."

"I'll see you sooner than that, won't I?"

"It's best I don't return. You know this has got to be all over the *Coconut Telegraph* by now."

"Then stay here with me."

"I can't, Lacey. There's still too much I've got to get into place if I'm going to pull off our disappearance. I'll come back for you after sundown Monday."

"Okay, but you better not leave my ass behind."

SATURDAY | 25 OCTOBER | 19:33 EST
Latitude = 24.5547, Longitude = -81.7963
Windsor Lane, Cruising Old Town
Key West, Florida

"She couldn't have simply vanished from the island," Roger said in frustration, slowly driving through the neighborhoods in search of his latest embarrassment.

Roger and Rosalyn had spent the entire day interviewing Lacey's friends and associates, to no avail, other than stoking the island's gossip mill. The town was abuzz with speculation, given the police were keeping tight-lipped as to the reason for their inquiries. Yet all were in agreement, it had to be something big, made even more intriguing by the Detective Morales involvement with the investigation of his ex-girlfriend.

"We'll find her," Rosalyn said. "And if you're asking for my input, I say it's time to release the story to the papers. We need the public's help."

"Unleash the Key West media machine? I can already see tomorrow's headline, *Morales's Folly: Girlfriend Wanted on Murder Charges*. Damn it, Roz, I knew there was something about her that kept me on edge."

"Don't blame yourself, Roger. That girl's sure got some smooth goin' on. She sure as hell fooled the both of us."

.62

Venturing out for what was likely my last night of relative anonymity on the island, I returned to a safe haven and favorite hideaway of many a wayward soul, the Chart Room. I came there to plot my escape, and my fate. A situation that called for the collaboration of a trusted friend. Kelley served as my preferred, and only, option.

"I must say, you certainly do know how to pick them." Kelley shook his head and mouthed, "Murder?"

"I know. She seemed all sweet and innocent, even dating a cop."

"Those are the most dangerous ones. Lucky you found out before—"

"She offed me?"

"That's a possibility," Kelley said.

"Maybe she's reformed herself over the past seven years."

"Right," Kelley said.

"Maybe not, huh?"

"Don't forget, she brought a gun on your first date."

"Good point."

"Now, there is another issue we should consider," Kelley said.

"What's that?"

"Your true love—Kendra."

"Why would you say that?"

"I see how you react by the very mention of her name. The stress fades from your face and a twinkle appears in your eyes. You're in love with that girl."

"Ever since I stopped judging her it's been different. Good different."

"Then what's the problem? Take her, not that crazy bitch."

"Kendra said she'd go, but I blew it off."

"Why?"

"I have to protect her. I can't draw her into a life on the run. That's not fair to her."

"And, the bigger issue?" he asked.

"Could it be I'm scared to death of commitment?"

"For a man to find true freedom, he must first free himself from the grip of his fears."

"Trying to change the outside world is a lot easier than changing the one inside," I said.

"True love can change anything, but you must give it your everything."

"You mean my full commitment."

"I do. Give her a choice and give her a chance. If she makes the decision to go, you'll be starting off on equal footing. Not a bad place to begin a new life together."

"Lacey's a safer bet, even if she is a killer. With Kendra, odds are she'll always be a runner."

"Sounds like someone is afraid of getting hurt," Kelley said.

"What about you, Kelley? Are you ready for a new adventure? There's always room for one more."

"Oh my, no. I've already lived my share of adventures. I came here to quietly live out my days."

"If you came, you'd never be homeless again. I've got the means to take care of both of us."

"You must understand, if it were as simple as grabbing hold of the chance for a better life, I'd have already latched on to it. In my mind, I deserve to be homeless."

"Kelley, no one deserves that."

"Don't you get it? That's why I'm in this situation. I haven't lived a perfect life. I've made more than my share of mistakes. I've hurt people. Worse, I've used them. This is God's way of punishing me."

"Cursing a life is the business of the dark side, not God."

"The dark side is where I spent most of my life."

"That doesn't mean you have to end it there, Kelley. Don't you see the goodness in you? I sure as hell do. That's why I've trusted you with my deepest secrets."

"You've certainly shown me I am of value to someone."

"Does that mean you'll come?"

"No. Like I told you, I came here to die."

We sat quietly sipping our drinks, each looking in opposing directions at nothing in particular. It was a time of reflection. Of appreciating our, albeit brief, shared life experience. Our connection of destiny.

"Kelley, I need your help with a few errands."

"Of course, whatever I can do."

"Here's the combination to the case," I said, jotting down the numbers on the back of a coaster. "I need you to pull out the photo album labeled 'Ski Vacations' and there, behind each picture, you will find five one-hundred dollar bills. I've made a list of equipment and supplies I'm going to need by Monday night." I slid the list in front of him. "Look it over and let me know if you see any problem getting everything on it."

Kelley studied the list, commenting as he read. "Snorkel gear, two of everything I see, a six-pack of camp stove propane, raw fish does become tiresome, okay, flashlights, water proof, of course. Now, wait," Kelley said looking puzzled upon reaching the bottom of the page. "What is a Sea-Scooter, in heaven's name?"

"Sea-Scooters are relatively new on the consumer market, but the government and military have used them for years. They're a personal underwater propulsion system. All you do is pull back the throttle and hang on tight. And don't get cheap ones, either. Top of the line models. Two of them."

"Will do. Everything on your list should be available at any of the marine supply shops on the island."

"I saw a West Marine a couple of blocks from the Cypress House. Head over there tomorrow to shop for these items. You'll need to have them hold the order for you until just before closing time Monday. Then grab a taxi with the stuff from West Marine and take it to the beach off Simonton Street, on the Gulf side. I'll come in by dinghy after dark for the pick up."

"Got it."

"I also need you to call this number in the morning to make arrangements with Captain Gus to get my personal belongings aboard the Gypsy Rose, including the case of my photo albums and documents."

"Anything else?"

"There is one more thing. The rest of the cash stashed in that album, keep it. Consider it my investment in your future."

"Jake, how splendid. I can't begin to thank you enough."

"No, Kelley, thank you. I could not have asked for a better confidant in Key West."

"Why do I have the feeling our paths will again collide somewhere down the road?" Kelley said.

"I trust you're probably right, my brother. Best if you always keep a couple extra minutes on that phone I gave you."

"I'll be looking forward to that call, Jake."

.63

"Good morning, angel." I said, standing at the foot of the bed.

The remainder of my night was spent walking the streets in solitude. With my escape plan set in motion, my thoughts had turned to matters of the heart. I considered my options, I battled my demons, and I finally faced my fears, only to be swiftly suspended by the news of the day. The front page headline prominently displayed in a street corner newspaper box seized my attention.

'Schooner' bartender wanted by Feds
on murder charges

Regarding my particular circumstances, the sub-headline was more personally damning.

*McKenna assumed on the run
aided by drifter accomplice*

"Angel, my ass!" Kendra shouted, quickly waking from a dead sleep. "What time is it?"

"Around five, I guess."

"I sure hope you didn't come here thinking you'd get one last piece of ass!"

"What's gotten you all fired up?"

"You, you bastard. Jerking me around like you do. You left me this morning without saying a single word."

"I didn't see the point. You were all pissy with me before you went to sleep."

"I was only pissy because you don't trust me," she said.

"Kendra, for real? Tell me why I should trust you with my feelings. Every time I let down my walls, you give me a damn good reason to put them back up."

"I know I do," Kendra said. "But I've changed. From the time I spent with you, I've learned what truly matters in life. Your love is the only thing that can make me whole. I can't lose you again."

I wasn't ready to talk about it. I didn't have the words. I needed sleep to give my subconscious mind time to mull through the choices I saw before me, while still battling the mystery of Kendra's sincerity. Even her ability to be sincere. Turning on the lamp, I tossed the Sunday paper on the bed.

"What's this?" Kendra's eyes focused on a blurred, video surveillance picture of me. "Oh, shit."

"It gets worse. Read the article."

As she read the story, Kendra periodically shook her head in dismay. "You had to go out with a bang, didn't you? You know, Oswald is going to kill you."

"I know. Literally."

"You've got to speak with him. That's the only way out."

"Wrong. There are better ways."

"He knows you've been staying with me."

"I figured. All the more reason to disappear as soon as possible."

"What about us? We've got to talk about this."

"We will. I promise. First, will you hide me a few hours so I can get some rest? I'm so tired I can't think straight."

"Of course. Climb on in here, you pain in the ass. I wonder why I let myself get mixed up with you in the first place."

"Being an expert profiler, I would suggest it has something to do with my irresistible charm and good looks."

"You are really something else, Jake Lander. I don't know why I can't resist you," Kendra said, pulling the sheet over our heads as she prepared to pounce, "but I can't."

.64

SUNDAY | 26 OCTOBER | 17:32 EST
Latitude: 24.5583, Longitude: -81.7874
KWPD Headquarters, Interview Room A
Key West, Florida

"Good afternoon, Detective Morales, Detective Chapman. I'm Oswald Reinbold, Domestic Operations Officer for the Central Intelligence Agency, and this is my colleague, Agent Kendra Carlin."

"Thank you for coming in to meet with us," Roger said. "I understand you have information which may assist us in the capture of Amber Uhrig, a.k.a. Lacey McKenna."

"Yes. However, our focus in this case has nothing to do with Ms. Uhrig. Your person of interest, Jake Lander, is of our utmost concern."

"See, Rosalyn, I knew that guy was trouble the moment I saw him."

"Your assumption may be quite accurate," Oswald said, "nevertheless, Jake Lander is one of our agents. Thus, the CIA will obviously be taking the lead. You understand, don't you, Detectives?"

"What about the FBI?" Roger said. "It's my understanding they've already deployed officers to assist. They'll be here in a matter of hours."

"They won't be joining us. Langley is abreast of our situation and I've been assured the Bureau will stand down, as a professional courtesy. The only individuals involved in this operation are the four of us in this room."

"Except for our chief, of course. You do realize we're required to get his clearance," Roger said.

"That won't be necessary. Your chief has been contacted by our Deputy Director, William Harvey, informing him, as I now inform you, this operation never happened. The three of you, your chief and you, Detectives, either collectively or individually, are never to discuss this operation or its outcome, as this is as a matter of national security. Is that absolutely clear?"

Obtaining a pledge of secrecy from Roger and Rosalyn, Oswald continued. "Upon completion of this operation, you will have Ms. Uhrig in custody, and Blake the drifter will simply have moved on. The CIA will handle the Jake Lander affair internally. Understood?"

They nodded in agreement, accustomed to the pecking order when the Feds were in town.

"Regarding Ms. Uhrig," Rosalyn said, "what do you have for us?"

"As for her whereabouts at the present moment, we have nothing. However, thanks to the exemplary efforts of Agent Carlin, who I must say has gone above and beyond, we have obtained the details of Lander and Uhrig's escape plan."

Oswald glanced toward Kendra in acknowledgement of her commitment. He could not determine if the expression upon her face was portraying humility or chagrin.

"So, fill us in," Roger said.

"All I can tell you at this point is our operation will take place tomorrow evening. Too, we will need the use of a patrol boat. Other than that, you will be provided additional details as the situation dictates."

"You must understand, this is a small town," Rosalyn said, "and this is big news for us. The Key West Police Department damn well better be showing a unified front on Uhrig's capture. Otherwise, the townspeople will assume she's getting off easy because of her involvement with Roger."

"You're absolutely right, Rosalyn," Kendra said. "Keep up the proper appearances with your community, the media and the people within your department. We can't afford to give the public any reason to question if there's something going on behind the scenes."

"It won't matter, they're going to anyway," Roger said. "This is Key West."

65

MONDAY | 27 OCTOBER | 11:47 EST
Latitude = 24.5610, Longitude = -81.8019
Schooner Wharf Bar, The Historic Seaport
Key West, Florida

The smallest of events on this little island are regularly transformed into grandiose affairs, as is the case of this year's Gypsy Rose send-off party. Dressed in full pirate regalia, Captain Gus and Rita acted the part of the belles of the ball. Moving about the bar as if celebrities, saying their good-byes, passing out kisses and collecting drink offers, they reveled in the limelight.

The Schooner Wharf's atmosphere was particularly festive for this hour of the day, even in the wake of Lacey's demise. Perhaps because of it. The chatter and speculation of her criminal past and mysterious disappearance swirling around the crowd only added to the excitement.

The Schooner Wharf Bar's resident magician and master of ceremonies, Magic Frank, stepped up to the microphone to make an announcement at the request of the Key West Police Department.

"If I could have everyone's attention, please. Excuse me. Everyone, quiet down. As we've all been talking about, the only thing we've been talking about, Lacey's disappearance has created quite a stir around town. The Key West Police need our help. They've asked I let you know there are officers posted outback here, on the boardwalk. Anyone who has seen or heard from Lacey since Friday night, please speak with one of the officers. The same goes for a drifter by the name of Blake. They don't have a last name. He's that guy who recently started hanging out here, mostly in the afternoon.

"Imagine that," a local shouted from the crowd. "That's Lacey's shift. I bet she knew that guy long before last week."

A roar of opinions rolled across the crowd.

"Listen up," Frank said. "There's more than a handful of theories being tossed around out there. Let's all hold our judgment and let the police do their job. And in case you haven't already heard, the FBI is offering a $100,000 reward for information leading to the capture of our infamous Ms. Lacey. No reward was offered for the drifter."

"Hand me that thing, Frank," Gus said as he made his way up to the stage. "I've got a few words."

"Okay, everybody. Let's have a round of applause for Captain Gus Matheson!"

The Schooner Wharf erupted in hoots and howls.

"That's enough. Quiet down. Alright. Rita and I want to thank you all for coming to our send-off party again this year. I realize it's almost twelve noon, our scheduled launch. Like last year, and come to think of it, every year, our departure is going to be a little behind schedule. I'm waiting on the UPS man. Soon as he gets here with my new solar panels, we'll be setting sail."

"Get to the point, Gus," Rita called out from the crowd.

"Before we go, Rita and I want to say, living on the hook, this bar has served as something of a living room for us. So we figure that makes all of you our family. We're going to miss you this winter. You're the reason we keep coming back to this odd little port. Thank you and we'll see you come May. Now, Rita, was that good enough?"

"That was fine, dear."

"Alright then, with the formalities out of the way, I better let Raven get back up here to entertain you folks. Besides, my glass is empty and looks to me, Rita's is, too. Who out there wants to buy us a farewell round? — How about you, Magic Frank?"

66

MONDAY | 27 OCTOBER | 23:59 EST
Latitude = 24.5196, Longitude = -81.9727
Aboard Unit A-03 of the KWPD Marine Fleet
The Florida Straits, South of Woman Key

"That's Woman Key off our starboard," Roger said, slowing the vessel to a crawl.

"This is perfect. Cut the lights," Oswald said. "The intelligence Agent Carlin acquired suggests they will cut through the channel just north of here. We'll stand-down until we get a visual on them."

"Oswald, would this be a good time for you to fill us in on our strategy?" Roger asked.

"Definitely. Let me repeat once again, the Central Intelligence Agency holds full authority, thus takes full responsibility for this covert affair. What that means to you, Detectives, you are expected to follow instructions precisely as given, and no questions. Understood?"

The detectives verbally committed to the conditions outlined by Oswald, while Kendra observed her beloved friend affectively don his old cloak of rigidity.

"With that said, the operation is quite simple. No weapons are believed to be on board their vessel. Besides, Jake would not be one to incur casualties once he knows he's caught. Additionally, there will be no radio transmissions. We will make contact via visual and audible communications only. Once contact has been made, we will pull along side their vessel to board and take our prisoners. Roger, you and Kendra will board their boat. Roger will bring Ms. Uhrig back to our vessel, and Kendra, you'll be responsible for containing Jake on the other boat."

"Yes, sir. Then I'll follow you back to port as we discussed."

"Prior to making land, however," Oswald directed his attention to the detectives, "we will rendezvous with Kendra so that I may join them. At that point, we will go our separate ways."

Roger was quick to scrutinize the process. "Why not board at the point of capture?"

"The Agency has a matter to address with Uhrig, which I will tend to once we have her in custody."

"What matter?"

"Roger. There will be no more questions."

"Yes, sir."

"Excuse me," Rosalyn said. "I've got a visual on a vessel, at two o'clock." She pointed in the direction of Boca Grande Key.

Roger grabbed the binoculars from Rosalyn's hand and focused on the boat. A sailboat. A familiar sailboat. "That's the Lucky Dog! What in the hell? Lacey's trying to escape using my boat!"

Kendra smirked. "Now doesn't that's just add insult to injury?"

"I'm going to get crucified by the press."

"And the guys in the department," Rosalyn said.

"People," a straight-faced Oswald said, "we have a job to do. Roger, proceed to intercept the Lucky Dog."

.67

"Almost home free. There's Boca Grande up ahead," I said. "Looks like we've dodged a bullet, or two."

Since slipping out of port, our voyage remained uneventful. A beautiful night on the water, the sky above was clear, the moon shown bright. In operations mode, I was mentally focused on the task at hand, maneuvering us to our rendezvous location.

Lacey's attitude was lighthearted, even manic, as she delighted in her sail to freedom. "You have no idea how good this feels. Particularly after being under house arrest all weekend. Thanks for getting me out of there, Jake. I can't even imagine what it would be like locked up in prison for the rest of my life."

I calculated our distance and speed, determining our exact time of intercept, as Lacey gleefully babbled non-stop.

"I'm going to miss Key West," she said. "I'll miss my friends, and the fun, and of course, the attitude. I became a different person while on that rock. I gained a sense of trust for people that I never had before. Even for myself. In a way, I became Lacey McKenna. She was a more compassionate and fun-loving me. Lacey would never have gotten mixed up in drug money. She was a kind soul who always looked for the good in others. I guess that's what I liked most about Key West. I found Lacey there. What about you? What are you going to miss about your old life?"

"Only one thing, really," I said, only to be interrupted by Lacey's fear-filled shriek.

"Look! Over there. We've got company."

I grabbed the binoculars to identify the boat. Steadying myself, I peered toward the vessel speeding our way.

"Tell me it's not the Coast Guard." Lacey said.

"Worse than that. It's the Key West police."

"What? How could they know where to find us? It had to be Gus and Rita. They're the only ones who knew. I trusted them!"

"People will do almost anything when it comes to money," I said.

"And I trusted you! You bastard. This is all your fault. If you hadn't dropped my backpack, none of this would've ever happened. You've ruined my life, you prick."

With the their vessel merely one-hundred yards from ours, strobes of red lights began skipping across the water, escorted by indistinguishable words echoing in the night air. Closing in, they slowed to make their final approach. The words from the loudspeaker became ever more clear.

"I repeat, this is Detective Roger Morales of the Key West Police Department. Anchor your vessel, immediately."

I complied and moved to the bow to drop anchor.

"Both of you, sit down with legs crossed. Put your hands behind your head." His words echoed across the water. "Do it now!"

Watching them inch closer to the Lucky Dog, guns drawn, I followed their orders. Lacey began sobbing uncontrollably. I pulled her down next to me in compliance to their orders. Reaching us, Rosalyn and Oswald positioned buoys between our vessels, tying-off the Lucky Dog.

"Prepare to be boarded," Roger said.

He and Kendra climbed aboard the Lucky Dog. Without hesitation, nor an ounce of compassion, Roger spun Lacey around, not saying a word as he cuffed her.

"Please, Roger. Don't do this to me. You've got to let me go."

He ignored her pleas.

"Could I use your handcuffs?" Kendra said to Rosalyn while still holding me at gun point.

"Sure thing, darlin'. Here you go."

Grabbing me by the arm, Kendra attached one end of the cuffs to the railing of the boat, leaving the other end for me. I watched as they maneuvered Lacey between the vessels, screaming and tugging.

"Excuse me, Agent Carlin," Roger said, pausing before returning to the police boat, the concern in his voice apparent. "Are you sure you know how to handle a boat? The Lucky Dog can be very temperamental."

"Relax, Detective. I've got it under control."

.68

"You can't do this to me!"

Roger led Lacey down below where he handcuffed her wrists to eyelets in a seat designed for just such a purpose. Not saying a word, other than her rights, Roger climbed back on deck to rejoin his colleagues.

"I have her secured."

"Then if you will excuse me," Oswald said, "I have business to attend to with Ms. Uhrig."

Grabbing the black duffle bag he had brought on board, Oswald squeezed through the narrow opening to reach Lacey in the cuddy. Pulling open the bag, he retrieved an iPod with full-sized, noise-canceling headphones attached. Placing the sensory limiters over her ears, he turned the volume to maximum. Pressing play, Pink Floyd's *Dark Side of the Moon* began to blare. Next, he pulled a small, black silk hood from the duffle bag, placing it over Lacey's head, loosely tying it off around her neck. Screaming violently, Lacey fought in an effort to free herself, jerking against the restraints. Taking a pen syringe from its protective sleeve, Oswald dosed her with a tranquilizer. Within seconds, Lacey fell calm and quiet. Oswald checked her pulse before returning to the deck.

"It sounded like you were torturing her down there," Roger said.

"I merely gave her a sedative. Disabling the captive is standard procedure while in the midst of an operation, and I was not about to listen to her ranting the entire way back."

"And it's going to be a long trip back to port with a sailboat in our convoy," Roger said. "The Lucky Dog can barely do five knots top speed."

Their slow pace allowed the roughening seas to toss the patrol boat from side to side as they droned toward port. Filling the time, Rosalyn shared a thermos of coffee, granola bars, and her impressions on their successful mission.

"That was a textbook example of stellar interagency collaboration," she said. "The CIA got their rogue agent and we have our fugitive. And, Roger, by bringing Lacey to justice, you've not only maintained your credibility, but also avoided another romantic tragedy."

"I'm still going to hear about it from the guys. Can you believe she used the Lucky Dog for her escape?"

Oswald, contributing to the banter, said, "The way I see it, you had quite a successful night, Roger. You got your man, or woman, and recovered a stolen sailboat. Not bad for a night's work."

"That's right, I did. Thanks, Oswald."

"Now that you've captured your agent," Rosalyn said, "may I ask, what's the future hold for him?"

"Jake will likely be transfered to Utah and detained indefinitely. I'd be surprised if he was ever to be released,"

Oswald said. "Ironic and quite sad, Jake ran to find freedom, yet all he achieved was imprisonment."

"What about you?" Roger asked. "Are you returning to Chicago right away?"

"Not anytime soon. I believe it best I stay put in Key West for now. I'm ready for a change of lifestyle and this island looks to be the ideal place to explore my options."

Rosalyn interrupted. "Pardon me, guys. Does it seem the Lucky Dog is lagging a bit too far behind?"

"And off course," Roger said. "If they maintain that heading, it'll take them directly into shallow waters. The Lucky Dog's draft would never make it through there."

"Perhaps there's a problem," Oswald said. "Flash the light to see if we can get a response."

Roger repeatedly flashed out messages in Morse code, to no avail. The Lucky Dog continued its path toward the trap of unforgiving sandbars.

"I'm going to swing around to cut them off," Roger said. "Hold on."

Making a rapid turn to the starboard, Roger sped directly toward the Lucky Dog. Closing in, he cut back the throttle, lunging their bodies forward, to maintain a safe distance and avoid the same potential trap of shallow waters.

"I can't see either of them," Rosalyn said. "They must have gone down below."

"I don't believe it," Oswald said. "They're probably down there fu—"

Before he could finish his words, in a brilliant burst of light, the Lucky Dog erupted in flames. Six consecutive localized explosions followed, ripping the boat apart, sending pieces of debris flying. With burning sections of the Lucky Dog strewn about, awestruck, the three stood in silence as Roger maneuvered their boat from harm's way.

"What in the hell just happened?" Rosalyn said, wiping smoke-filled tears from her eyes. "Roger, take a wide swing around the debris field." She scanned the surrounding waters with the searchlight. "I don't see them out there, anywhere."

After an extended search, making endless passes among the still flaming shreds of the Lucky Dog, Roger said, "I hate to say it, but I don't see how anyone could have survived that blast."

"No one could have," Oswald said. In a calm and calculated tone, he concluded, "Better they be buried at sea. It's so much cleaner for the Agency that way. Continue to port." He pulled out his phone and began to dial. "Excuse me, I need to inform Langley."

He stepped aside to watch the dimming flames off in the distance as he listened to the phone ring.

"Reinbold here, sir. Our loose ends have been tied up." Oswald smiled upon receiving accolades from the other end of the line. "Thank you, sir. I am truly honored. . . . I agree, given the circumstances, it is by far the best possible outcome. . . . I'll give that serious consideration. . . . You're right, this may be the ideal time."

Oswald knew his life would be far different, now that his colleagues and, sadly, his only true friends were gone. He faced a defining moment. His entire life, as well as his very identity, were on a collision course for a new reality. Thankfully, one of his own choosing.

As he watched the flames fade away, Oswald bid his friends farewell. With a tear in his eye, he bestowed on them his blessing.

> *May you be eternally bound in love. The way it was surely meant to be. Know you are forever in my heart, Kendra, Jake. I place my trust in the heavens above that one day we will meet again.*
>
> *Perhaps La Habana.*

.69

"Now that was a blast," Kendra said as she pulled the snorkel mask from around her head, shaking free a wet mop of mocha hair.

"I'd say. That was one hell of an explosion."

"I was talking about the Sea-Scooter ride, silly."

We had made it out of harm's way, safe, sound, and most of all, free. My exhilaration in the moment was not for myself alone, nor was my escape. The demise of Agent Jacob Lander was undoubtedly best for everyone. His knowledge of the formula to control the individuality of thought would be forever lost to death. From the Agency's perspective, far better lost forever than lost to the enemy. From mine, it freed me from their chains, granting me the chance for a new life. One of my own choosing.

"I've never felt so alive!" Kendra said, pulling me in for a kiss. "We're free, baby. They don't own us, anymore."

"You realize what this means, don't you?" I said, holding her tight. "We're stuck with each other now."

"I figure that's what it was going to take," she said.

"What? Left with no other choice?"

Uninhibited by city lights, the moon drew a brilliant line that shimmered across the ocean to the beach where we stood. As if illuminating the path before us, my time had come to surrender, trust and believe. Standing there in the soft sand of Boca Grande Key, Kendra by my side, I found the clarity of thought I had forever sought. I was finally free from the world's intentions, and no longer imprisoned by the past. — Mine or Kendra's.

"That's not true, at all," I said. "I've had a lifetime of options to choose from, but none could keep my interest. Once I stopped the madness, the only truth I desired was one that includes you."

For once, I felt my feelings were real.

"What now, Jacob?"

"A new beginning, and a clean slate. The Gypsy Rose should only be a couple hundred yards around the shoreline. I'm ready if you are."

"What's your hurry? The moon tonight, it's so romantic. That, and I've never done it on a beach."

"A virgin, huh? I prefer a woman with a little experience, but what the hell, I'll take you just the way you are," I said, ripping off her sopping wet clothes.

"You are so bad, Agent Lander."

"I love you, too, Agent Carlin."

.epilogue

You could say I'm living proof—a dead man can rise from the ashes to create a life anew.

Walking out of the surf that night, for the first time in my life, I felt I truly knew the real Jake Lander. A man I had not encountered for decades, a man I had finally come to trust. Thankfully, my journey to freedom and truth was not in vain. I found them both at *the end of the road*.

Reflecting on the time I spent in Key West, the days of my self-reconciliation, I realized that, too, I had come to surrender to a quiet urging from within. Trusting the spirit that reminds, *You shall know the truth, and the truth will make you free,* was the only option that remained.

The way I see it now, end of the road, or the beginning, it's simply a matter of perspective.

At the center of my newfound passion for life is Kendra. Together, we have learned to put the past behind us, so to fully embrace each new day. With her in my world, every moment is an adventure. Just the way we like it.

Regarding Lacey, Amber Uhrig now lives about 100 miles east of Los Angeles, at the Victorville Federal Correctional Complex. Found guilty on all counts, the likelihood of her looking me up any time soon is slim. I genuinely feel bad that she lost her freedom. There is nothing worse. Who could have imagined that her offshore account would have made me such a filthy-rich, happy man.

And finally, from here, the other side of the Florida Straits, I must confess:

Key West is as cool as they come, but amigo, Havana happens!

ABOUT THE AUTHOR

Kevin first visited the island of Key West in the 1980s, became entranced by her fantastical allure and funky charm, leaving him with the dream of someday making that tropical paradise his home. The decades to follow were a blur of business and pleasure, accompanied by the responsibilities such escapades demand. Growing weary of the *high life*, Kevin dropped from the radar to pursue the freedom that can only be found in the *simple life*. Today, his longing fulfilled, Kevin lives in Old Town Key West and is a naturalized citizen of the Conch Republic.

Also by Kevin May ❧ Eden: A Novel

Made in the USA
Charleston, SC
14 May 2013